To Tom and Beth
V Bill Rudrick(?)
I Co. 15:58

Not Beyond Reach

Not Beyond Reach

Stories for the Family

V. Ben Kendrick

REGULAR BAPTIST PRESS
1300 North Meacham Road
Schaumburg, Illinois 60173-4888

Cover photo, background: H. Armstrong Roberts
Cover photo, inset: Baptist Mid-Missions
Cover design: Laura Short

To the many friends who stand faithfully with us in the ministry of missions. Words can never fully express the heartfelt appreciation that Nina and I have for this very special group. It is both a joy and a privilege to dedicate this book to them.

Library of Congress Cataloging-in-Publication Data

Not beyond reach.
  1. Christian fiction, American. I. Title.
PS3561.E4233N68 1988 813'.54   88-3071
ISBN 0-87227-124-2

NOT BEYOND REACH: STORIES FOR THE FAMILY
© 1988
Regular Baptist Press
Schaumburg, Illinois
Printed in U.S.A. All rights reserved.

Second printing—1992

I wish to thank Sallie McElwain and Lynne Tanner for their help in the preparation of this manuscript. Their editing, proofreading and typing are sincerely appreciated.

CONTENTS

Foreword 9
Introduction 11
To God Be the Glory 13
Mr. Stone's Request 19
Unpredictable Life 23
Timely Awakening 27
That Next Door Neighbor 33
Caring Dorm Mother 39
Jocko's Song 45
A Blessed Response 49
Sweet Will of God 55
That Turkey Dinner 61
A Glorious Change 65
It's Your Life 71
Kidnapped for Good 77
A God of Miracles 83
Trusting God for the Future 89
The Stranger 93
The Backyard Tire Swing 97
For My Good 103
Tara's Love 107

The Seventh Hole   111
Eyes but Can't See   115
Distant Singing   119
A New Beginning   125
Good out of Bad   129
Lost   133
Something very Special   137
Love and Care   143
Unpleasant Blessing   147
The Reason Why   153

FOREWORD

Suspense. Surprises. Challenge. Answers to prayer. These are just a few of the exciting words that describe *Not Beyond Reach* by V. Ben Kendrick. The stories related by Brother Kendrick concern people, but they also have to do with snakes, warthogs and even a parrot that speaks three languages!

Ben Kendrick is a man rich in Christian experience. After twenty-one years of missionary service in the Central African Republic, he was called to the home office of Baptist Mid-Missions to serve as coordinator of deputation. I have been particularly impressed by his leadership in Men for Missions, a challenging work confronting the men in our local churches with the great and glorious opportunities for men in the realm of worldwide missions. Ben writes out of this wealth of service, leadership and personal evangelism.

Not Beyond Reach is a book about people, and Ben knows people. He has done the cause of Christ a great service by remembering experiences with people and by relating them so interestingly with his pen. The overall impact upon me as I read these stories was one of gratitude to God for the marvelous way He reaches people and saves them and then uses them to reach still others. The reader of these accounts will surely be stirred to tell others of the crucified, buried, risen Son of God. Teachers and preachers will also find in this book a wealth of illustrations.

>Paul N. Tassell, Ph.D., Litt.D.
>National Representative
>General Association of Regular
>Baptist Churches

INTRODUCTION

In this day when all moves so quickly, and somehow we get caught up in the almost unbelievably fast change in the world, we need to be brought back to the reality and truth of the Word of God.

The Word of God does work. As so often is said, "The Word of God stands the test of time." We need to see in the practical areas of life that faith, trust and obedience to the Bible continue even in this modern age.

Possibly such truth is seen best in those experiences of missionaries in areas with which we are not familiar. They seem to bring us back to simple reality. You cannot improve on everyday life experiences. This book will give you the opportunity to see the practicalness of the Word of God in your daily life.

Ben Kendrick needs no introduction. He has lived many of these experiences. The Lord has enabled him to see in everyday life on the mission field the truths that come from the Word of God. The Bible is practical, it is useful and, to the one who knows Christ, the Word breaks forth many times each day. Often we do not take time to see this or we take it for granted.

Allow yourself the luxury of identifying with the experiences of the people in these stories as they see God's Word work in their lives. These experiences, however, will only be enjoyable and entertaining when you also realize that God works the same way in your life. For you, this book should end up being enlightening.

Not Beyond Reach is the product of a missionary who constantly sees that God's Word works. When the Word works, it produces faith. So this book should increase your faith, not just for the large areas of life, but in the everyday experiences.

Read, enjoy, but also, dear reader, apply. Let the eyes and ears of Ben Kendrick be a practical help in your life.

William A. Brock, D.D.
State Representative
Ohio Association of Regular Baptist Churches

TO GOD BE THE GLORY

The sudden shouting outside the hospital sent a chill through Dr. Don Sears, who was standing beside the operating table. He gripped the scalpel tightly as he strained to catch the people's words. Only two days before, a group of disgruntled rebels had come onto the mission station and threatened the lives of everyone if they were not given food.

"Have the rebels returned?" asked the missionary doctor. His eyes narrowed with concern as they peered out over his face mask.

"Paul," he called to one of the medical students, "take a look outside and see what's going on."

The young African hurried to the door, only to be met there by another student who was coming to give the doctor a message.

"Andrew is back, Doctor!" the excited student shouted through the screen door. "The truck just came around the bend down the road."

"Thank the Lord," whispered the mission doctor. "It's a miracle he made it." The two-thousand-mile trip to the coast was extremely dangerous because of the civil war that was raging all over the country.

The veteran missionary spoke heartily to his operating team, "Just a few more minutes, my friends, and this fellow can be taken back to the ward."

Don Sears was in his twentieth year of service and had

seen the hospital work develop from its beginning. Now it was not unusual for the doctor and his team of American and African nurses to treat up to four hundred patients a day.

Don stripped off his rubber gloves and headed out of the building to join the growing crowd in the yard. In minutes, the entire nearby workers' village had emptied out to welcome Andrew back from his long trip to the coast.

"Hello, Andrew," called the mission doctor. "It's so good to see you back safely. Any problems along the way?"

The tall Sara tribesman stuck out his hand to clasp the hand of his missionary coworker. The tribal scars across his face wrinkled as he smiled.

"I had trouble only once, Dr. Sears. Several gunmen blocked the road about four hours from here. They asked me my name and my destination. When I told them I had medical supplies on the truck, which they would have found out anyway, they became very excited. Some of them talked about shooting me and taking the truck for themselves. It was a very dangerous situation in which I found myself, and I really prayed that God would perform a miracle and spare my life."

"How did you get free from them?" questioned the doctor.

"Another truck came along at that exact moment. The gunmen thought that the approaching truck was loaded with rebels from another group, and they fled into a nearby forest."

Andrew smiled as he pointed to a bullet hole in the side of the truck.

"I guess this is proof of what happened back there on the road. The rebels did not want me to go free, and one of them fired at me as he was disappearing into the brush. The bullet just missed me and hit the truck right here." Andrew stuck his finger into the bullet hole.

"Within seconds I was in the truck and getting away as fast as I could make it move."

The people roared with laughter—part of which was

relief— as Andrew acted out his escape.

That evening, Andrew, his wife Ann and their three children ate dinner with Don and Jane Sears. During the meal Andrew did most of the talking, describing the three-week-long trip to the coast.

"When you get rested from your trip, Andrew, we need to send some grain up to Pastor James. A runner arrived today with a message from him. For the first time in years, he is seeing people dying from starvation. They have eaten their seed crop for next year's planting."

Andrew put his hand to his mouth. "Oh, Dr. Sears, I forgot to tell the rebels that I had grain on the truck. Thank the Lord for that oversight. I'm sure they would have shot me right then and there had they known that I was hauling food." The hospital worker laughed as he spoke.

"Sometimes the Lord causes us to forget things!"

That night, a number of men volunteered to unload the truck, knowing how quickly it was needed to carry sacks of grain to the village where Pastor James lived. By eight o'clock the next morning, Andrew, along with several hospital workmen, was ready to set out on the 150-mile trip.

Ann and the children waved good-bye to Andrew as he maneuvered the truck out of the driveway onto the dirt road that ran alongside the mission station. To take advantage of the free transportation, two Bible students with their families and all of their belongings were on top of the load. The people waved and shouted to each other until the truck was out of sight. Ann and the children walked slowly back to their hut, saddened to see their loved one depart so quickly again. They knew, however, that no time could be wasted in getting the grain to Pastor James.

Don and Jane Sears talked until late that night about the work in general. Their hearts were heavy not only for the Christian people, but for the entire population suffering because of the famine throughout their land.

The clapping of hands outside caused Don's eyes to fly

open and he sat up in bed with a start.

"Who is it?" he called out.

"It's David," came the reply. David was the night watchman for the station. "I have bad news, Dr. Sears. Come quickly."

Don slipped out from under the mosquito net, grabbing his flashlight from underneath his pillow. He dressed quickly as Jane, too, awoke and sat up in bed.

"What is it, Don?" she asked.

"I don't know," responded the missionary doctor. "David is outside and says he has bad news."

Opening the front door, Don saw David and three other men standing there before him.

"This is Gapo, Dr. Sears. He just arrived on his bicycle. He told me that Andrew has been shot along with our Bible school students and the workmen. A rebel band has stolen the grain and burned the truck."

Don Sears stood motionless in a state of shock. His years of experience told him not to panic.

"Has Ann heard the news about her husband?" he asked David.

"As far as I know, Doctor, no one has told her. Only the four of us know what happened. I was sitting by my fire with John and Noah when Gapo arrived with the news. We came directly to your house."

"Noah," instructed Don, "go and tell Ann to come immediately to my house. Don't tell her what happened. Just say that I have something to tell her."

Noah turned and disappeared into the darkness. Don invited the three men into the house and began making some coffee for his guests. Within a matter of minutes, Noah had returned with Andrew's wife. She looked frightened as she entered the house. Jane Sears offered her a chair and sat down beside her.

"I have some news that you must hear," said Don, looking at Ann.

"I know what you are going to tell me, Dr. Sears. I had the feeling when Andrew drove away this morning that I would never see him again here on earth. Please tell me what happened. I am ready to hear the story."

Don then turned to Gapo and asked him to describe what had happened. As Gapo spoke, Ann sat with her head bowed and her hands folded in her lap. Tears ran down both sides of her face. Finally Gapo stopped talking and Ann looked up at her missionary coworkers.

"I take this from the Lord. Andrew and I have had a very happy life together. God has given to us three beautiful children, and all of them know and love Him. Andrew's heart was in the work. He wanted more than anything else in his life to please God, no matter what he had to do to bring that about. I know that I will never see him again on this side of Heaven."

Ann paused and then smiled as she continued. "But, Dr. and Mrs. Sears, I really mean it when I say that it isn't such a bad thing to die for Jesus. My Andrew was given the privilege by the Lord to make the ultimate sacrifice—to give up his life."

Without hesitation, Ann turned to Gapo and asked if he was a Christian. The African responded that he was not, although he knew what Jesus had done for him. Ann proceeded to talk to the young man while the rest of the friends silently prayed. Within minutes, Gapo dropped to his knees beside the chair where Ann was sitting and said that he wanted to accept Jesus as his Savior. Gapo prayed, with Ann's help, then Ann stood to her feet and took the young man by the hand. Jane wiped her eyes as she listened to her Christian sister.

"My Andrew is in Heaven tonight," Ann said, "but I want you to know that I am rejoicing with the angels in Heaven because of Gapo accepting Jesus as his Savior. This one conversion, dear friends, is worth it all. I know that Andrew would have said the same thing. To God be the glory."

MR. STONE'S REQUEST
(Based on a True Experience)

I really don't see how we can pay that repair bill," murmured Betty Walters as she fingered through the pile of monthly bills lying on the table before her. "We just can't handle emergencies like this, Bob."

Earlier that week their six-year-old car had broken down, requiring extensive repair. Just that morning Bob had received word from the garage that it would cost them $500.

"I understand what you are saying, honey," said Bob, concerned over their need for $500 and the use of their car. "Only a miracle of the Lord can help us through this one."

The young couple sat in silence for a few moments until Bob spoke again.

"Well, we can thank the Lord that the garage has permitted us to take the car for now, although we must pay them within a week."

Bob and Betty had been married for four years. A year after their marriage, God had called them to Bible college to train for His service.

"If only we were done with school," Betty sighed. "It seems that this last year has been the hardest yet. Well, I shouldn't complain. At least your job at the shoe store provides enough for us to pay our bills."

"That's right," Bob agreed. "The Lord has supplied our needs. I'm sure, too, that somehow He will provide the $500 next week to pay the garage."

Later that evening as Bob and Betty were looking through their Sunday School lessons, they talked again about their financial need.

"Remember how I used to take you out for dinner at least once a week right after we got married?" Bob smiled as he remembered. "Now I can count on one hand the number of times that I have taken you out to dinner the past three and a half years."

"Well, we really haven't missed it, have we, Bob?" responded Betty pleasantly. She always seemed to come up with the right answer at the right time.

"No, I guess not," answered Bob. "But, honey, I would like to treat you to something special now and then."

The young couple exchanged smiles and then went back to studying their lessons. The ring of the phone startled both of them.

"I'll get it." Bob hurried across the room. "Why, hello Aunt Mary," he said, surprised. "This is really something to hear from you. What's the weather like out there in California?" Bob paused as he listened. Then, "You say you mailed it two days ago? That's wonderful, Aunt Mary! Betty and I sure do thank you. It should be here Monday or Tuesday. Thank you, Aunt Mary. We're praying for you too."

Bob put down the phone and stood for a few moments before returning to his chair.

"What is it, honey?" asked Betty, anxiously awaiting the news.

"Aunt Mary sent us a check for $300," responded Bob. "She said lately she had been thinking a lot about us here at school and felt she should send some money to help out."

The young couple got down on their knees beside their chairs to thank God for the $300 miracle gift which was already in the mail to them. The excitement of the phone call had stirred their hearts. They recounted to one another how God had supplied their every need from the time they entered Bible college.

The next morning the young couple's conversation was again dotted with comments about the faithfulness of the Lord.

"Dear Father," prayed Bob at the breakfast table, "thank You for Aunt Mary's phone call last night. It was just what we needed, Lord, to encourage us to trust You for this need we face. Thank You, dear Lord, for how You are going to supply that need."

"Isn't it wonderful," sighed Betty, holding her Bible tightly in her hands, "to know that God knows every detail of our lives. I'm so ashamed of the times that I haven't trusted Him."

The pastor's message that Sunday morning was entitled "God's Answer." Bob couldn't help believing that the Lord had given Pastor Smith the message especially for them. While he and Betty stood at the back of the auditorium, thanking the pastor for his message, one of the elderly men who had been a member of the church for many years stood nearby waiting to speak to them. Cyrus Stone's wife had died twelve years before. His clothes were out of style and well-worn, and he was regarded as one who did not possess very much in the way of material wealth.

"Hello, Bob and Betty," Mr. Stone greeted them, as he fumbled inside his coat. Finally he pulled out a sealed envelope. "I know this sounds strange, but during the night God awakened me and asked me to give this to you."

"Well, thank you, Mr. Stone," replied Bob, taking the envelope and shaking the man's hand. He placed the sealed, soiled envelope in his inside coat pocket.

"Now, I want you to promise me one thing, Bob," smiled Mr. Stone. "I want you to treat Betty to a dinner at Parker's."

Almost everyone in the area regarded Parker's restaurant as an excellent eating place. The couple was surprised at Mr. Stone's request. They were sure that he did not eat at Parker's and wondered if he even knew the cost of the meals there. As they were going down the front steps of the church, the elderly gentleman called to them.

"Whatever is left over, you can use for any need you might have."

As they got into their car in the parking lot, Betty and Bob both were intensely interested in the contents of the envelope. Driving away from the church, Bob handed Betty the soiled envelope. Quickly she tore it open and gasped as she looked inside.

"Oh, honey," she exclaimed, her eyes filling with tears, "you won't believe what's in here." She reached into the envelope and brought out two one hundred dollar bills and a fifty dollar bill.

"We've got money to pay for the car and $50 left over," said Bob, his voice filled with emotion.

"We sure have." Betty was equally touched with what had happened the evening before and now that morning at church.

"But remember, honey," she said smiling through her tears, "you owe me a dinner out of this—a dinner at Parker's restaurant."

UNPREDICTABLE LIFE
(A True Story)

Let's stop for something to eat, Dad," I suggested as I saw the sign in the distance for gasoline and food. We had been traveling since nine o'clock that morning, and my stomach was telling me that it was time to eat.

"That sounds all right to me," answered my 75-year-old father, sitting beside me on the front seat. Little did Dad realize how much of a joy it was for me to have him in the car with me. We planned to have him spend a week or two with Nina and me in Cleveland.

It was just one week before that I had become very burdened for my father. My mother was called home to be with the Lord two years before, leaving Dad a very lonely man. As I thought about my father that day, I decided to invite him to Cleveland to spend some time with us. As soon as he picked up the phone and started talking, I knew that Dad was very depressed.

"It's too far for me to drive, Ben," he objected. "I don't think I'll come out."

"But, Dad, you won't have to drive a bit. I'll come out and get you and when you're ready to go home, I'll take you back home."

"I don't think I'd better do that," countered Dad. "That's a long way for anyone to drive."

Knowing that Dad loved baseball, I thought of the

California Angels who were scheduled to play the Cleveland Indians in a few days.

"I'll tell you what we'll do, Dad. Let me come and bring you out, and then while you're here, we'll go see the Cleveland Indians and the California Angels play a game. I'll get tickets right behind the dugout. How do you like that?"

"Well . . . ," replied my Dad rather slowly, "okay, come and get me."

The following week I made the trip from Cleveland to Shickshinny, a small town on the bank of the Susquehanna River in eastern Pennsylvania. Dad lived in an apartment near the center of town. I arrived in the evening; the following morning we were on our way to Cleveland. Once Dad was in the car, he seemed excited about the trip to Ohio and his visit with us.

"Here you are, Dad," I said as I passed a large piece of pizza to him. He looked at it and smiled. I knew Dad was enjoying himself. After our little picnic there along Interstate 80 in central Pennsylvania, we continued on our way. I drove along at a comfortable speed enjoying the time with my father.

About 5:30 that afternoon we arrived in Richmond Heights, an eastern Cleveland suburb. Nina had the evening meal ready for us, since I had telephoned ahead, telling her approximately the time of our arrival. After the meal was over I turned to Dad.

"The stadium is off in that direction," I said, pointing toward the city.

"Where is Lake Erie?" asked Dad, knowing that the stadium was near the lake. His excitement about seeing a major league baseball game was mounting. As he prepared for bed, I told him that I probably wouldn't see him in the morning as I went to the office rather early.

"I'll call you sometime tomorrow," I called to Dad as we said good night.

It was the next afternoon when I called Dad. "I'll be home about 5:30," I said. "Just as soon as I change clothes, we'll go down to the ballpark."

"Whatever you say, Ben," said Dad cheerfully. "I'll be

ready and waiting for you when you come home."

At 5:30 sharp I walked into our apartment. Dad sat there with his jacket across his lap waiting for me. His excitement was contagious—I could hardly wait until we started for the stadium. Dad and I had never gone to a baseball game together before, due largely to my many years in Africa. Even during my furloughs, my schedule had been very heavy with meetings.

It took me just a few moments to change from a suit and tie to something more casual for the ballgame. Dad talked all the way down to the ballpark. I could tell he was enjoying himself. We parked and walked into the stadium.

"This is the largest major league baseball park," I told Dad. "It holds around eighty thousand people." Once we were in our seats, I noticed that Dad was busy studying the ballplayers. There they were right before him—those he had watched perform on television so many times. Once the game started, the computerized scoreboard with the many characters moving across the screen captivated Dad's attention. The Indians weren't doing very well; about the eighth inning I looked over at Dad, who was completely engrossed in what was going on on the field.

"Dad," I said, "I think they are too far behind to catch up. Maybe we ought to leave now and get ahead of the traffic."

Dad looked at me, rather surprised. "Well, if you want to go, then we'll go."

I knew by Dad's answer that he wanted to see the game to its end. We did just that. It was a joy to my heart to see Dad enjoy himself to the fullest, watching a major league baseball game. The game over, we walked to the nearest exit from the stadium and slowly made our way to the car in the parking lot.

Dad was talking baseball. We got into the car and Dad was still talking about baseball. I wound my way down through the parking lot, with Dad talking about the ground ball that the Cleveland shortstop had allowed to go through his legs.

"He's no ballplayer. Why, he never even touched that ball." Dad was replaying the game for me.

I was just pulling out onto the street from the parking lot when I heard my dad sigh. I looked at him, thinking he was tired. I put my arm around him and asked him if he was all right. He stayed in that position for two or three seconds and then his head bent forward onto his chest. There was a groan and Dad was in Heaven.

Not realizing that my father had gone to be with the Lord, I put my arm around him, thinking that he was possibly unconscious and alive.

"Hold on, Dad, I'll get you some help in a moment." Across the narrow street was a policeman.

"I need help!" I called. "I think my dad has had a heart attack." I parked alongside the road, and the policeman opened up the door and began pushing on Dad's chest. I took a blanket out of the trunk of the car and laid it on the ground. By that time, more policemen had arrived and Dad was placed on the blanket face up. Mouth-to-mouth resuscitation was started. As they continued to press upon his chest, I bent over and looked into Dad's face. That was when I realized that his Heavenly Father had promoted him to Glory.

It was difficult for me as I went home that night without Dad. But as I looked into his empty bedroom and saw his Bible on the stand beside his bed, my heart cried out with praise to God that I'd had a Dad who loved Him and lived for Him. Standing there, I realized that one of my most faithful prayer supporters was gone—taken without a moment's warning. The awesome truth came home to me that life passes quickly and is so unpredictable.

TIMELY AWAKENING
(Based on a True Story)

"The drain to Miss Crawford's shower is unclogged, Mr. Daily," called the African workman. Beth Crawford, one of the teachers at the school for missionary children, had complained to Bob that morning of the blocked drain in the house she shared with the station nurse, Ann. She had asked her coworker if one of the station workmen could clean it out for them.

"That's great, Ngara," answered Bob, the veteran missionary. "Don't forget to replace the screen over the drain."

The African workman clicked his tongue, indicating that he had heard. The water from the shower ran out the drainpipe onto the ground where it rapidly soaked into the soil. Seeing Bob through the classroom window, Beth went to the door to ask about the clogged drainpipe.

"Everything is fine, Beth," Bob assured her.

"Thanks, Bob," responded the smiling teacher. "Ann and I are looking forward to you and Ginny coming tonight for dinner. Bring your appetites with you! We're going to have your favorite dish."

Bob Daily knew what Beth was talking about. It was the time of year when the Africans gathered a certain kind of mushroom. The large mushroom was a meal in itself, but when it came with a buffalo steak, there was nothing that could compare with it, as far as Bob was concerned.

That evening Bob and Ginny arrived at six o'clock as planned. The aroma of steak and mushroom filled the little bungalow where Beth and Ann lived. Before long they were at the table enjoying the dinner while relating the events of the day.

The evening passed quickly; at nine o'clock Bob glanced at his wristwatch and then over to Ginny. "Well, it's about that time," he said, getting to his feet. "Lights out in fifteen minutes." The station's electric generator ran nightly from 5:45 to 9:15.

The couple thanked Beth and Ann for the nice evening and made their way to the car. "We could have walked," Bob commented, "but I just don't enjoy sharing the road with snakes."

Only two nights before he had shot and killed a seven-foot black spitting cobra just outside their back door.

Shortly after they arrived home, Bob went out to the motor house to shut off the electric generator. With the flashlight on the path before him, he returned to the house to get ready for bed. Ginny had lit a kerosene lamp to provide some light. The veteran couple was well aware of the scorpions, centipedes and other such creatures sharing the house with them and thankful for the protection of the mosquito net surrounding their bed.

They had just dozed off to sleep when they heard someone clapping his hands out in the drive. Bob pulled his flashlight from underneath his pillow, lifted the mosquito net and walked over to look out the screened window.

"Who is it?" he called.

"It's me, Jonathan," came the voice. "Miss Beth wants you to come right away. She says bring your gun. There's a snake in her bedroom." In minutes Bob was dressed and was on his way with Jonathan, the night watchman, to the girls' house. As they walked into the house, they found the two girls sitting in the living room with a kerosene lamp between them.

"This is a fine thing to do," admonished Bob, trying to look serious. "A guy works hard all day on the station, and now I'm called out to shoot a little snake."

"It's not very little, Bob," protested Beth, trying to hide her fear. "I woke up with a strange feeling that a snake was in the room. I turned on my flashlight and immediately saw it. There's a green mamba curled up on the nightstand beside my bed. I sure made an exit out of there in a hurry."

Jonathan had gone to a shed behind the house and come back with a long-handled rake. Together, the two men very gently began pushing open the bedroom door. "There it is, Mr. Daily," whispered Jonathan, pointing to the large mamba snake covering the top of the nightstand. "It sure is a big one."

Bob and Jonathan both knew that they were within eight feet of one of the most aggressive, poisonous snakes in the world. Bob kept his flashlight directly on the snake. He knew that he would have to act very quickly, since one bite from the mamba could mean death.

Bob estimated the snake to be nine or ten feet long. He had seen Africans die from snakebites and knew what a horrible death it could be. He wanted to take every precaution possible.

"Let me hit it with the rake, Mr. Daily," whispered Jonathan.

The mamba raised its head about two feet off the nightstand as the two men watched. They both stood motionless, wondering what the snake would do next. Mambas had been known to crawl with over half of their body raised above the ground.

Beth and Ann, sitting in the next room, nearly jumped out of their chairs at the blast of the shotgun. Bob had just raised the gun to his shoulder, aiming at the snake, when without any warning the huge mamba sprang toward the light. The scatter shot riddled the front of the mamba's body, which practically fell at the feet of the two men. They both quickly stepped out of the room and closed the door behind them, fearing that the snake might still be able to bite.

"What happened?" demanded Ann. "Did you get it?"

"It leaped at the flashlight," answered Jonathan. "Thank the Lord that Mr. Daily had his gun in position, or one or both of us could have been killed. The snake hit the floor right at our feet."

"Is it dead?" Beth quavered.

"We're not sure," answered Bob. "I know I hit it about a foot behind its head, but whether it's still able to bite or not, I don't know."

The men waited a few minutes, then slowly opened the door. There lying on the floor was the dead mamba. Beth gasped, putting her hands to her face as she looked at her would-be killer.

"To think that snake was only two feet from me while I was sleeping," exclaimed Beth.

"Let's take a look and see how the mamba got into your house," spoke Bob as he headed for the shower room that separated the two girls' bedrooms.

Bob took one look at the drain and gave a low whistle. "There's your answer," he said, pointing to the open drain hole. Ngara had forgotten to put the grid over the drain.

"Well, it's really not all his fault, Bob," Beth confessed. "I took a shower after class today and never even noticed it."

Bob smiled. "Isn't God wonderful to us? We have so many life-threatening dangers about us. I guess now and then He allows things to happen to increase our awareness of the dangers of carelessness."

Bob had prayer with the two girls before returning home. "Thank You, Father," prayed Beth, "for sparing my life tonight. I know it was foolish of me to be so careless. You are so kind, dear Lord, to protect us even in spite of our own thoughtlessness at times."

Before he left, Bob helped the girls put up mosquito nets over each bed. Meanwhile, Jonathan scrubbed the bedroom floor, washing away any evidence that the mamba had been shot. He smiled, however, as he looked up at the wall above his head. There were pellet holes through the lampshade as well as marks on the wall. "That will be your clean-up job, Mr. Daily. After all, you're the one who shot the gun."

Upon hearing his remark, the three missionaries broke out in laughter, thankful to the Lord for His protection and relieved that the mamba episode was over.

THAT NEXT DOOR NEIGHBOR
(Based on a True Experience)

I don't ever want to see that woman in this house again!" Judy Burns threw the dishtowel she was holding against the wall. "Every time she gets around me she talks about Jesus." Judy glanced out the window to see her neighbor, Rose Young, walking through the vacant lot separating their houses.

Rose had been saved two years before, after living a very wicked life. For eight years she had worked as a dancer in nightclubs and had also been addicted to alcohol and drugs. Then, while walking in Chicago one day, Rose met one of her high school friends, Debbie Oaks. They began talking about their lives since graduation. Rose related her experiences, hiding very little of her past.

Debbie listened in silence while her friend spoke. Finally Debbie was able to tell of how one day a friend had called her to invite her to a meeting."

"She said it was a missionary conference being held in her church," Debbie remembered. "My friend told me that I would hear some fascinating stories about how missionaries lived and worked among primitive people. That evening I went with her to the meeting."

As Debbie talked, Rose intently listened to every word.

"The middle-aged woman who spoke at the conference was a nurse. She told how she rode a bicycle through jungle paths for hours at a time to get to the villages in order to treat the lepers. I cringed as I listened to her talk. It was difficult to imagine the woman standing before me exposing herself to such a dreaded disease and a lonely life in the jungles."

Rose slowly shook her head at what was to her an amazing story.

Debbie continued, "The missionary described how she would bathe the ulcers and clean the lepers' sores. She mentioned that helping the people gave her the opportunity to tell them about Jesus and how He died on the cross that they might have everlasting life."

While Debbie spoke, Rose thought of her own life and how she, too, needed that same Savior. Although not a physical leper, Rose realized that she was a spiritual leper in the eyes of God.

"At the close of the service," Debbie said, "I went forward and accepted Christ as my Savior."

The former high school classmate then shared with Rose how God had changed her life completely. He not only had given her eternal life, but He had brought many friends into her life who believed as she did. She pulled her billfold from her purse and showed Rose a picture of her husband. "He is my greatest friend on earth. It was only two weeks after I was saved that the Lord led Jim and me together. We knew immediately that we loved each other." In telling of their beautiful relationship, Debbie assured Rose that it was all because of Christ, Who was not only their Savior but also in the center of their home.

Rose had never heard a more beautiful story. She reached out and put her hand on Debbie's shoulder. "I need Christ as my Savior, Debbie. I need His help in my life too." The two women stepped into a nearby alley and there, with their heads bowed, Rose Young confessed her sins to God and asked Christ to become her Savior.

Now, approximately two years later, Judy and Allen

Burns had moved into the vacant house next door to Rose Young. Judy had no idea of the kind of life that Rose had once lived. All she knew was that Rose was religious and wanted to tell others about it.

Upon entering her house, Rose knelt beside her bed. "Dear Father," she prayed, "Judy needs You so much. Please, Lord, help me be a witness to her. Help her see herself as a sinner and receive Christ as her Savior." Rose felt in her heart that some day she would have the joy of seeing Judy Burns become a sister in Christ.

A week went by, but nothing much happened between the two women. Judy seemed to sidestep Rose whenever she could. The following Saturday afternoon, Rose and Judy were both shopping in a nearby grocery store when they nearly ran into each other at the end of one of the aisles.

"Hi, Judy," said Rose, smiling, "we nearly collided."

"We sure did," responded Judy with only a half smile.

"Say, Judy, are you and Allen busy tonight? I'd love to have you come over and try out my new chocolate chip cake recipe."

It was Allen's night out for the bowling league, and Judy knew that she had no plans except to stay home. Something inside urged her to accept Rose's invitation.

"Well, as a matter of fact," she spoke hesitantly, "Allen is going bowling tonight, and I was going to stay home and read."

"Why don't you come over, Judy? You're a good cook. You'll be a good judge for this new recipe."

Judy laughed at Rose's remark.

"OK," she agreed, "is 7:30 all right?"

"That's just perfect," responded Rose.

That night Judy arrived at 7:30 sharp. Within a few minutes she felt more comfortable in Rose's presence than she had at any previous time. The two women sat and talked about a number of things. Judy declared Rose's cake an overwhelming success. Their friendship seemed to grow by the minute.

Well into that evening, Rose decided to approach Judy once again regarding her spiritual needs.

"Judy, can I share with you something about my past life? I'm not at all proud of it, but I really would like to tell you about it."

"Only if you want to, Rose."

Rose then related how she had been a nightclub dancer for years. She told how she had gone through days of deep depression and turned to alcoholic beverages and drugs to help her through those times. She smiled as she recounted meeting Debbie Oaks on a street corner in Chicago. She told practically word for word her conversation with Debbie. Judy sat spellbound as Rose told how she had bowed her head that day, standing there in the alley with Debbie, and received Christ as her Savior.

"My life was changed immediately, Judy. My nightclub days were over. The drinking and drugs completely disappeared. My language changed. I began attending a church where the Bible was believed and taught. My love for God has grown, and I try to live my life completely for Him."

"You mean to say that Jesus can do that for anyone who accepts Him?" asked Judy.

"Oh yes, He can," said Rose.

"Now I understand," said Judy, half laughing. "Now I know why you persist in talking about Jesus."

"He loved me so much that He died to save me," affirmed Rose. "That's why I want to tell others about Him."

Judy sat in silence. Finally, she looked up. "I do understand, Rose, I really do. I know that Allen will think I'm crazy, but, Rose, would you pray with me and help me to accept Jesus as my Savior?"

The two women knelt beside the couch in the living room. There Judy asked Christ to save her.

"I feel like a different person already," Judy murmured.

"You are a different person, Judy," said Rose, drying her eyes. "Now you must pray that Allen will accept Christ."

As she got to her feet, Judy put her arms around Rose and hugged her.

"Thank you, Rose, for inviting me to test that chocolate chip cake. It was well worth the visit."

CARING DORM MOTHER

Laura gripped the back of the pew in front of her. It was all she could do to control the overwhelming anger within her.

"I hate this place," she whispered to herself. "Why did Mom and Dad insist that I come here?"

The speaker in chapel that day was a missionary from Africa. He described in detail how many of the African Christians were persecuted because of their stand for Christ. The more he spoke, the worse Laura felt. She knew that she had not been living for the Lord and had violated some of the rules of the Christian college she was attending. She thought of the unsaved fellow at a nearby state college whom she was secretly dating. Her studies, the college rules, her fellow students and the daily chapel services were all upsetting her. She was relieved when the closing prayer was finished and she could leave the auditorium.

Instead of going to her scheduled class, Laura walked to the edge of the campus and started down the main street of town.

"I've got to get out of this place," she said to herself. "I can't stand it any longer."

She walked to a phone booth in the center of town and dialed the dorm where her boyfriend, Mark, lived.

Unsuccessful in contacting Mark, Laura slowly made her way back to her room in the dormitory. Mrs. Wicks, the dorm mother, spotted her as she entered the dorm.

"Not feeling well, Laura?" she called, knowing that Laura had a class.

"I have a bad headache, Mrs. Wicks," answered Laura as she continued down the hall.

The dorm mother made no attempt to follow. Laura entered her room, threw her books on the desk and flung herself on the bed. She burst into tears and began pounding the bed with her fists.

"Oh, I hate this place," she cried. "I feel just like a prisoner!"

The disturbed young lady laid there for some time before falling asleep.

"Laura," spoke the soft voice. "Laura, are you in?" Laura opened her eyes, feeling better now that she had forgotten her troubles for at least a little while.

"I'm here, Mrs. Wicks," she answered, getting to her feet and going to the door. Opening it, she saw the kind dorm mother standing there with a smile on her face.

"Can I come in, Laura?" she asked.

"Sure, Mrs. Wicks," responded the student.

The middle-aged woman entered the room and sat down on one of the two chairs. She sat for a moment in silence and then looked at Laura.

"I hope I'm not intruding, Laura, but I just felt I should come and see you. Is there something troubling you, Laura, with which I can help you?"

Laura looked at the floor and burst into tears.

The dorm mother moved over to the bed where Laura was sitting and sat down beside her.

"What is it, Laura? Can you share it with me?"

The distraught student sat for some time with her head in her hands. Mrs. Wicks patiently waited until Laura wanted to speak.

"Today in chapel I could hardly wait for it to be over. I don't like this place, Mrs. Wicks. I hate it!" said Laura, as she buried her face in her hands again.

The wise dorm mother just sat and listened as Laura talked.

"I feel awful inside, Mrs. Wicks," sobbed Laura. "It

seems as though I have lost my love for the Lord and for His Word, and I don't even think of the spiritual needs of others anymore. Something has happened to me, Mrs. Wicks, and I can't understand it. I'm afraid to say anything to Mom and Dad when I call them."

Mrs. Wicks waited a bit and then began to speak.

"Is it a fellow, Laura? Is there some man in the picture?"

"Why do you ask that?" queried Laura, looking up at the dorm mother.

"I've been around for many years, Laura, and have talked to a lot of girls about all kinds of things. Somehow I think that the reason for your unhappiness could be a man. Am I right, Laura?"

The young lady hesitated for a moment, then admitted, "Yes, there is someone, Mrs. Wicks. His name is Mark, and he is a student at State."

"Is Mark a Christian, Laura?"

The penetrating question startled the young lady.

"No, he's not, Mrs. Wicks. He's an atheist. He's been telling me a lot of things on our dates."

"Then you've been dating outside of campus rules."

"Yes," responded the tearful student. "I have been seeing Mark. I met him when I was out shopping one day."

"Let me ask you one more question, Laura," spoke the dorm mother in her pleasant voice. "Do you remember when you started feeling like this?"

Laura sat a moment and then looked up with a half smile on her face.

"It all began when I started dating Mark. That's when it started, Mrs. Wicks. Why didn't I see this before?"

"It's because you didn't want to see it, Laura," replied the older woman. "You see, dear, you wanted Mark more than anything else in the world and were willing to sacrifice things which had become very precious to you, including the joy of living as a Christian ought to live."

"Oh, Mrs. Wicks," said Laura, putting her arms around the dorm mother, "you're so wise. You remind me of my mother."

"Well," suggested Mrs. Wicks, smiling, "maybe it's because I've raised three of my own like you. I ought to know something about your feelings by now."

The dorm mother then prayed with Laura.

"Mrs. Wicks, I know this may sound silly, but do you think I could come to your apartment this evening after Mark is back in the dorm and use your phone to call him? I would feel better if you could hear what I say to him."

"You sure can, honey," agreed the older woman, patting Laura's shoulder. "You just come any time. I have no plans to be out this evening."

That night Laura went to make the phone call. Her hand shook as she pushed the numbers.

"Hello, may I speak with Mark White, please?" She looked at Mrs. Wicks and whispered, "He's in his room, and they are going to get him."

"Hello, Mark," said Laura. "No, I can't. I really can't, Mark," she spoke into the telephone. "Well, it's like this, Mark. I can't see you anymore. Do you remember on our first date I told you I was a Christian and tried to talk to you about the Lord?"

There was silence in the room as Laura listened to Mark.

"It's all over between us. It's not right for me as a Christian to date you. Mark, God does exist. I know it's hard for you to believe this of me, but He has saved me and has given me eternal life. He has directed my life up to the time I met you. Mark, I love the Lord. Jesus is my Savior. I pray that some day He will be your Savior too."

Laura listened for a minute and then softly said, "Good-bye, Mark. Good-bye. I'll be praying for you." And with that she hung up the phone.

"Thank You, dear Father," she whispered, bowing her head. "Thank You for Mrs. Wicks, who helped me to come back to You."

The dorm mother sat by silently, wiping the tears from her eyes, thankful for the ministry that God had entrusted to her in being a dorm mother for girls like Laura. Before returning to her room, Laura hugged Mrs. Wicks and planted a kiss on her cheek.

"I can hardly believe all that has taken place today and the change in my thinking!" She hesitated and then smiled as she continued, "I'm really looking forward to chapel tomorrow."

JOCKO'S SONG

Ngoro, have you seen Jocko?" called Eric from underneath the car. He was changing the motor oil for a visiting nurse.

"I haven't seen him at all this morning, Mr. Bond," answered the African workman. "The last I saw your parrot was when I left the mission station last evening to go home."

Eric made his way up the steps out of the car pit. He picked up a nearby rag to wipe the oil off his hands.

"Well, I saw him last night around nine o'clock when I went out to the laundry house. Jocko always perches on a pipe just outside the door," spoke the saddened missionary. "I hope he has not been caught by an animal," continued Eric.

"Or stolen by somebody," added Ngoro.

The African's remark startled Eric. "Do you really think that someone would steal Jocko, Ngoro?" questioned the missionary.

"I know they would, Mr. Bond," answered Ngoro. "Jocko is a good talker. Why, he can speak three different languages. I've heard him speak English to you missionaries and French to the French people who visit you, and every morning he greets me in our African Sango language. Someone can get a lot of money for that bird."

The conversation between the two was interrupted by

a call from Edith Bond. "Eric, I need a few items from the store. Could you go to town for me?"

"I've just finished with Mary's car, honey. Give me a few minutes to wash up and change my shirt, and I'll be on my way," responded Eric.

Upon entering the house, he shared with Edith Ngoro's theory about the parrot being stolen. "He seems quite sure that someone took Jocko to sell him. I sure hope we can find him. He's such a nice pet and so friendly to everyone."

"Besides," added Edith, "Jocko really belongs to Penny, and she'll be home from school in a week. We could never get her another parrot like Jocko."

Eric washed up and put on a clean shirt. "Maybe I'll take Ngoro to town with me. He can look around the streets while I'm in the store. Who knows? He might just find Jocko."

A short time later, Eric Bond pulled up in front of one of the grocery stores in the small African city. "You walk around a bit, Ngoro, while I'm in the store."

The two men parted. Ngoro immediately headed down one of the side streets looking for any sign of Jocko. He passed two men selling African Gray parrots but knew that neither of the birds was Jocko.

Reaching the end of the street, he turned the corner. "Penny," called the familiar voice. "Penny, Eric, hello," came the words from inside a house. Ngoro stopped in his tracks and listened. There were a few whistles and once again he heard the parrot talk. "Edith! Edith!" came the voice. There was no doubt in Ngoro's mind that the voice belonged to Jocko.

He hurried back to the store. Even though he was tempted to look around at the many items, he instead searched the aisles for Eric and finally spotted him.

"I found Jocko, Mr. Bond. I heard him speaking your name. It's really him."

Eric headed straight for the checkout counter. "Let's go," he said to his African friend.

The two men hurried to the house where Ngoro had heard Jocko's voice. They saw a French woman looking out one of the windows when they arrived.

"That's the house, Mr. Bond. Jocko's voice came from that house."

Eric walked to the front door and knocked. The same woman they saw in the window appeared.

"Good day, Madame," spoke Eric in his best French. "My friend tells me that he heard a parrot here in your house speaking my name. Do you have such a bird?"

The young lady smiled. "Oh, yes, Monsieur. We do have an African Gray parrot. I just bought him this morning from a street vendor at the market."

She invited Eric into the house. His eyes immediately settled upon the large gray parrot with a bright red tail. It was Jocko.

"Edith!" called the parrot.

"Edith is my wife's name," explained Eric, walking over to the cage. "My daughter's name is Penny."

"Penny!" repeated Jocko.

The parrot then began to whistle. Eric smiled as he stood and listened to Jocko hit every note perfectly.

"What is that tune that he whistles?" asked the French woman. "He has been whistling that same tune since I brought him home."

"Oh, that's a little song that we sing at our house. It's called 'Jesus Loves Me,' " Eric answered.

The woman laughed, "You have a religious bird, Monsieur."

"By the way, I'm Pastor Eric Bond and I live at the American Mission on the edge of the city limits," spoke Eric, extending his hand for the usual handshake.

"Pleased to meet you, Pastor Bond," replied the woman. "I'm Madame La Porte. My husband is a school teacher."

She asked Eric if she could keep the parrot until her husband returned home from work that afternoon. She then promised to bring Jocko to the mission station that evening.

"Of course you can," agreed the happy missionary. "Please plan to stay for a piece of cake and a cup of coffee. My wife and I would appreciate it if you would do

47

that. We would like to get to know you."

Upon his arrival back home, Eric told Edith the amazing story. "And just think," he grinned, "Jocko was used of the Lord to make this contact with an unsaved couple."

Mr. and Mrs. La Porte arrived with Jocko after the evening meal. When Eric offered to pay them the money they had paid the street vendor, they refused to accept it.

"We would like to know more about that little song you taught your parrot," spoke Mrs. La Porte. "I'm sure not many African Grays whistle religious tunes."

The four of them laughed at the remark. Eric then proceeded to tell about the words and their meaning. He shared with them his conversion to Christ and what the Lord meant to him.

"Does Mrs. Bond believe the same as you?" questioned Mr. La Porte.

"Oh yes," replied Edith. She then gave her testimony of how she had received Christ as her Savior.

"This is all so wonderful," exclaimed the French woman. "Where does that put Jacques and me? Do we need to accept Jesus like you did to get to Heaven?"

Eric continued to witness to their new friends. Jocko sat quietly in his cage as though he knew what was being said. Finally about midnight, the French couple asked Eric to pray with them. Convinced they needed to be saved, both confessed their sinfulness and asked the Lord to forgive them and make them His children. The two couples then talked about the Christian life and its responsibilities.

As the La Portes stood up to leave, Jocko burst forth whistling "Jesus Loves Me." Eric and Edith had never heard him whistle so well. He hit every note perfectly.

"Thank you, Jocko," whispered Mrs. La Porte. "Yes, thank you, Jocko," echoed her husband. "You will never know how God used you and your song to help us."

A BLESSED RESPONSE
(A True Story)

Ben looked up from his desk to see one of the office secretaries standing in the doorway with a serious look on her face. She held a small piece of paper in her hand.

"Hello, Joyce," said the mission executive. "What can I do for you?"

The secretary held out the paper as she spoke.

"None of the men are back from the conference yet, Dr. Kendrick. I know that you just arrived from off the road, but we have received an important telephone call which I believe you would want to know about. A man in DuBois, Pennsylvania, called to say that a friend of his, also from DuBois, is in the Cleveland Clinic."

Ben listened intently as Joyce spoke.

"The man who called, Jeff Wheeler, is a Christian. He is concerned about his friend, who learned today from the doctors that he has cancer and is not expected to live."

"What is his friend's name?" asked Ben, making notes of the conversation.

"Bill Caster," replied Joyce, looking at the piece of paper in her hand. "Jeff says he knows of Baptist Mid-Missions and would appreciate it if one of the men here would go over and talk with Mr. Caster, who is not a Christian."

"I'll go over right now," Ben responded, walking over to take his coat off the hanger. He picked up a pocket-size Bible and slipped it in the inside pocket of his coat.

"Thank you, Dr. Kendrick," called Joyce, as she returned to her desk.

Ben left the office and was soon at Cleveland Clinic. He could not help wondering what the man he would soon meet would be like.

"Dear Father, help me," he whispered as he entered the room.

"Hello there." Ben hesitated, not knowing which of the two men who occupied the room was the right one. "I'm looking for a man by the name of Bill Caster."

"I'm Bill Caster," spoke the man in the bed near the window. "What can I do for you?"

"Bill, you don't know me, and I've never met you. My name is Ben Kendrick, and my office just received a call from Jeff Wheeler from DuBois."

"Oh yes," Bill responded. "Jeff and I worked together for years. He's a good friend."

"Mr. Wheeler just called to ask one of us from the office to come visit you," continued Ben.

"Well, thank you."

In a matter of minutes, the two men were engaged in conversation. Ben decided to keep the discussion away from Bill's serious condition. Even though Bill welcomed Ben, the veteran missionary sensed that there was a hesitation on the sick man's part to accept him. He asked permission to read the Bible and pray. Somewhat reluctantly, Bill agreed.

"Thank you, Bill," said Ben as he was about to leave the room. "By the way, I told you that my wife and I spent twenty-one years as missionaries in Africa. Well, I have a book in the car, coauthored by us, about Africa. Would you like to have it?"

"Sure," Bill assented, showing more friendliness.

Ben hurried out to the hospital garage for the book and was back in Bill's room within fifteen minutes.

"Thank you," Bill responded as Ben handed him the book.

"You're welcome, Bill. By the way, would you mind if I came to see you tomorrow?"

"Not at all," replied Bill. "As long as you have the time."

The next morning, Ben went back to the hospital. Upon entering the room and greeting Bill, he noticed that Bill had read halfway through the book he had received the day before.

"So, you and your wife actually were missionaries in Africa?" questioned Bill, looking somewhat surprised at Ben.

"That's right. The Lord gave us twenty-one wonderful years there."

The two men became engaged in conversation again, and even though Bill seemed more friendly than the day before, he still was a bit reserved. Sensing this, Ben asked if he could read the Bible and pray with him. When he finished, Bill told Ben that he was returning to Pennsylvania the next day.

"Do you mind if I come to see you before you leave?" asked Ben.

Bill had a half smile on his face as he answered. "It's all right with me if you have the time to come."

The next morning, Ben was at the hospital. Each day he sensed a better attitude on Bill's part. They talked for a while and then Ben pulled his chair up close to the side of the bed.

"Bill, I'd like to talk to you about something which is very important."

"What is it, Ben?"

"Well, this is the third day that I have come to visit you. The first two days before I left, I read the Bible and prayed with you, and I want to do that again today."

"That's fine with me, Ben," said Bill with a smile on his face.

Ben reached out and touched Bill's arm. "Bill, I want to tell you about my Savior."

A serious look came over Bill's face as Ben began.

"The Bible tells us a lot about God's love for us and how He provided eternal life for us through His Son,

Jesus Christ. He died on the cross for our sins."

Ben went on to relate that although he had attended church as long as he could remember, he did not accept Christ as his Savior until the age of eleven. He told how much Christ meant to him. Bill grasped Ben's hand and began to cry.

"I know what you are talking about, Ben. This is not new to me." Bill wiped his eyes and waited a moment before he spoke again. His voice trembled as he talked.

"I was the chairman of the deacon board at our church. I taught a Sunday School class of boys. I was very faithful in going to church." He hesitated again. "But I did it all in unbelief."

Ben looked at the face before him, covered with tears.

"Bill, let me ask you a question. Do you know where you will spend eternity?"

Again, Bill began to cry. "No, I don't know."

"Would you like to know for certain that God is your Heavenly Father, Jesus His Son is your Savior, and Heaven is your home forever?"

"Yes, I would," Bill whispered. "I really would like to know that."

Both men bowed their heads as Bill asked God to forgive him for his sins and to save him. Ben then followed with a short prayer. When he had finished, he looked at his friend.

"How do you feel, Bill?"

"I feel clean inside," responded the new Christian. "I feel that a change has taken place inside of me."

Bill went back to Pennsylvania that day. There was a phone call by Ben and an exchange of several letters before the last piece of correspondence came. Bill had dictated the letter to his wife when he was on his deathbed.

"I want to thank you," the letter related, "for what you have meant to me. My life has been beautiful since I accepted Christ as my Savior. I have perfect peace within me knowing that I will be with Him. Thank you, Brother Ben, for the part that you had in it all."

Several weeks later, Ben received a phone call one night from Bill's son.

"I'm calling to tell you that my dad has died. Even though I don't know you, I want to thank you for the three months of happiness that my dad enjoyed because of your influence on him. The last three months were the happiest days of his life. He died in peace."

Ben used the opportunity to witness to Bill's son, sharing with him that he, too, could be assured of a place in Heaven by accepting Christ as his Savior as his father had done. As Ben put down the phone, he bowed his head and cried tears of joy.

"Thank You, dear Father, for giving me the opportunity to tell Bill about You. Thank You for saving him."

The veteran missionary wiped his eyes and whispered to himself, "And to think that it all happened because of my response to a phone call."

SWEET WILL OF GOD

The men's quartet had just finished singing the last word of "Sweet Will of God." Lois Ames sat with her eyes glued to the morning sermon topic in the bulletin, "Not My Will, but Thine Be Done."

Lois and Jack Shaw had been engaged for just one week when Lois was diagnosed with acute leukemia. The words of the hymn ran through her mind.

> Sweet will of God, still fold me closer,
> Till I am wholly lost in thee;
> Sweet will of God, still fold me closer,
> Till I am wholly lost in thee.

A tear dropped on her open Bible. She glanced up at Jack, the first tenor in the quartet, whose light blue eyes were fastened upon her. She thought of Jack's words to her just that morning when he had picked her up to take her to church.

"We both know, Lois, that unless the Lord performs a miracle, we will not have a life together as husband and wife. We do know, however, that He has put within our hearts a love for each other. Our engagement will remain, Lois, until the Lord, Himself, sees fit to terminate it."

Lois, upon hearing the decision of the doctor, had immediately called Jack and suggested to him that they break off their engagement for his sake. Deep within her, however, she was glad to hear that the engagement would continue until the Lord intervened to end it. As far as Lois knew, this might be the last service that she would attend in her home church. She was scheduled to enter the hospital that afternoon.

Lois Ames, from the time that she was a child, had had a difficult life. Her father was killed in an automobile accident when she was ten years old. Two years later her mother, at the age of thirty-three, died unexpectedly of a heart attack. The only child in the family, Lois went to live with her father's oldest brother and wife. Her treatment from them was almost more than the young girl could bear. Her uncle, who was a drunkard, made it clear that Lois was unwanted in their home and often beat her in his anger. She came home one day from school to find her suitcase and belongings on the front porch. Her aunt came to the door and told her that she had to find some place else to live. Weeping, Lois gathered up as much as she could carry and started down the street, not knowing where to go. A neighbor two houses away, who happened to see and hear what was going on, went out to meet her. Putting her arm around the weeping girl, the middle-aged woman took Lois into her house.

"Why are you doing this for me, Mrs. Birch?" asked Lois, wiping the tears from her eyes. "I hardly know you folks, other than to say hello to you when I see you."

"We know more of what has gone on than you realize, Lois," Mrs. Birch smiled. "My husband and I for some time now have wanted to ask you to come and live with us, but we were afraid that it might cause trouble with your aunt and uncle. You see, Lois, we lost our only daughter when she was sixteen years old. She was coming home from a football game with some of the young people from our church. The car in which she was riding was struck by another car. The doctor said that Debbie never knew what happened. That's her picture over there." Mrs. Birch pointed to the picture on the wall.

"In fact, Lois, you remind us of our Debbie. Not only by your appearance, but also your voice sounds like hers."

"Mr. Birch and I are sad over the death of our Debbie, but we are not angry. You see, Lois, Debbie was a Christian. She accepted Jesus as her Savior when she was just a little girl. We believe that our lives are controlled by the Lord, and the things that happen are not mistakes, but are known entirely to Him. We do not question the Lord at all for what He allowed to happen to our Debbie. She is in Heaven with Him today."

Lois had never heard anything like that before. How could they love the Lord so much that even the death of their only daughter would not make them angry with Him? Lois realized immediately that there was a relationship that she knew nothing about between the Birches and the Lord.

Mrs. Birch accompanied Lois to her aunt and uncle's house to pick up her remaining belongings which were on the porch. The next day her aunt and uncle found out that Lois was only two doors away.

"It makes no difference to us," growled her uncle, "as long as she stays clear of us."

Lois found life very enjoyable with Mr. and Mrs. Birch. They could not have treated her any better. Her room was decorated in her favorite color, light blue. She had never experienced anything so nice. She immediately became one of the family, helping with meals, doing laundry, shopping and anything else she could do. Lois Ames had found a home.

Two weeks after Lois moved in with Mr. and Mrs. Birch, she went forward at church on a Sunday evening and received Christ as her Savior. Until then, she had not thought that she could be any happier, but she soon saw that Christ was the answer in her life. Upon her graduation from high school, Lois received a beautiful watch from her adopted parents. As she left the platform and started up the aisle, she stopped long enough to kiss them. As far as Lois was concerned, she was the happiest girl on the face of the earth. Christ was her

Savior and she had a wonderful home in which to live.

The church wanted to do something special for their graduating seniors and decided to pay for a banquet at one of the restaurants in the area. Lois was thrilled when one of the young men in the church, Jack Shaw, asked her to the banquet. The first date led to others, and the relationship between Lois and Jack was looked upon with favor by the church family. With financial help from her adopted parents, Lois enrolled in a Christian college. During her senior year she became ill and was told by the college doctor to return home for further tests. It was during this emergency time home that Jack asked Lois to marry him after her graduation from college. A week later, the tests showed leukemia.

Lois was admitted to the hospital that afternoon. She made it a point to tell each one who visited that her life belonged to the Lord and she wanted, more than anything else, for His will to be done concerning her. The twelfth day of her confinement, the hospital called the Birches and asked them to come. Pastor White and Jack were notified by Mr. Birch to go to the hospital. Lois was extremely weak and very pale when they arrived. She could hardly talk above a whisper. She smiled as she looked up into the faces of her loved ones. She squeezed Jack's hand, motioning him to bend over her so she could talk to him.

"Jack," she said in her ever pleasant, but now very soft voice, "the Lord is soon going to take me. You are the only man I ever loved. Honey, I want you to sing our favorite song for me."

In his beautiful voice Jack Shaw began to sing. Lois's eyes sparkled as he voiced the beautiful words.

> Sweet will of God, Still fold me closer,
> Till I am wholly lost in Thee;
> Sweet will of God, Still fold me closer,
> Till I am wholly lost in Thee.

Pastor White's heart was deeply touched as he spoke at Lois's funeral. "I felt at that moment when Jack sang that I was as near to Heaven as I could possibly be while still here on earth. Our beloved Lois Ames closed her eyes in death fully believing that was God's perfect will for her."

THAT TURKEY DINNER
(Based on a True Story)

Well, that does it," exclaimed Brad, as he sealed the envelope. "I hope this letter gets through to the Smiths."

Brad Coons, veteran missionary to the small landlocked central African country, was referring to the several mail carriers who in recent months had died attempting to bring the mail into the tiny government post. The local official had explained to Brad that the carriers, who had to travel for several days by foot and canoe, had been killed by lions.

"It would be nice if Rob and Ruth could be with us for Christmas," said Nan wistfully, watching her husband put the stamp on the envelope. "That is, if they can make it over the roads by then."

The roads which were closed in June by high water usually dried by November or December. Not only had Rob and Ruth Smith been classmates of Brad and Nan's in Bible college, but they also had all been in Paris together for French language study.

Brad and Nan had learned the tribal language quickly. They also had learned to live off the land like their African friends. Little by little they were introduced to food that they had never seen or tasted before. One day Nan was given a basket of small finger-like roots by one of the Christian women.

"These are our potatoes, Mrs. Coons," the woman smiled. "They grow wild in the jungle."

They didn't quite taste like potatoes, but Brad and Nan soon became accustomed to them and used them frequently in their meals.

A red plant with wax-like leaves was crushed to make a sauce which not only looked like cranberries but tasted like them.

In three weeks Brad and Nan received a response from the Smiths. "Thank you for your invitation to spend Christmas with you. We gladly accept. It will be good to see you again."

One week before Christmas, Rob and Ruth Smith drove into the mission station. "There are still a lot of holes in the road," Rob told them, dusting himself off as he stepped out of his pickup truck, "but it wasn't bad."

"Where's that turkey, Nan, that you've been hiding to feed us for Christmas?" he continued, smiling. He knew there was no such thing as a turkey in that part of Africa. Besides, the area was populated with all kinds of African game, so it would not be a problem for Brad to shoot an antelope for their Christmas dinner.

"I wish I knew where she put that turkey, Rob," replied Brad, winking. "We have the cranberry sauce and the stuffing, but those will look out of place with an antelope roast."

"Which won't taste like turkey either," agreed Rob, laughing.

"All right you fellows," interrupted Nan. "Ruth and I can prepare a good meal, but I'm afraid I can't work miracles. No turkey this Christmas."

The following day Brad and Rob took several of the African Christians and drove to the plains. They spotted a herd of antelope too far away to shoot. The men became excited when a huge warthog darted out of the brush in front of them and ran across the road, stopping some two hundred feet away.

Brad stopped the truck, took his gun and stepped out on the road. He aimed at the huge beast, which had turned to look at them. The bullet found its mark; the big, ugly animal ran about fifty feet and dropped.

"You've got him!" called one of the men in the back of the truck. The Africans immediately jumped to the ground and ran to the warthog.

"I've never seen one of these before," Brad admitted. "I've seen pictures of them in books and read about them. I guess they can be pretty mean at times." The missionaries and their African companions hoisted the animal into the back of the truck and headed back to the mission station.

"A pig!" cried Nan, teasing. "Why, I thought we could at least have a buffalo roast."

Brad cut off a hind leg and gave the rest of the animal to the African Christians to share.

"You mean you're not going to hunt for anything else?" asked Nan.

Brad shook his head. "Let's have a pork roast for Christmas. We've tried a lot of other things since we've been here. There's no reason why we shouldn't try this."

A special service was held on Christmas morning with about eight hundred people crowding the small mud-block, grass-roof church building. The African children recited verses and poems that they had spent weeks memorizing. Brad preached the morning sermon, and after greeting their many African friends, the two couples returned to the house.

"I smell something cooking," said Rob, as they approached the small brick dwelling.

"And it doesn't smell like pork either," added Brad.

"Well," said Ruth, "you may all think I'm crazy, but I think that smells like turkey."

They all laughed at Ruth's remark. The women began to get the food ready for the table. Rob and Ruth were excited about tasting their first African "cranberry sauce." As the two couples sat down for their Christmas meal, Brad gave thanks to the Lord for His provision to them and also for allowing the couples to be together.

All eyes were on the warthog roast as slices of meat were cut from it.

"If I didn't know better," Rob commented, "I would say that this meat on my plate was cut from the breast of a turkey."

He cut a piece and put it in his mouth. The look on his face was enough to tell the others that the taste matched Bob's words. All four agreed that a turkey could not have tasted any better. The warthog could not have tasted any more like turkey if it had been an actual turkey.

For the evening meal, Nan and Ruth made "turkey" sandwiches served with side dishes of "cranberry sauce" along with steaming cups of "coffee" brewed from a wild coffee plant found in the jungle. After the meal, they sang Christmas carols and Brad read from the Scriptures of the birth of Jesus. Rob ended the short devotional time in prayer.

"Thank You, Lord, for even giving to us the desires of our hearts to have meat that tasted like turkey for our meals today. It may sound unimportant to others, but, Father, we know that You did something special for us today, and we thank You."

The next day Rob and Ruth left to return home. As Ruth was getting into the truck, she turned to Brad and Nan with a big smile.

"It was wonderful to be with you," she asserted. "And, Brad, thank you for shooting that turkey."

A GLORIOUS CHANGE

The howling wind had already drifted the snow nearly five feet high against the building. Rod James looked over at his wife June sitting beside the small pot-bellied coal stove located in the middle of a one-room shack. A darkened kerosene lamp and the red glow of the burning fire cast eerie shadows about the dimly-lit room. Empty beer cans were scattered about. June sat motionless, staring at the bare plywood floor.

"I can't go on this way, Rod," spoke June with slurred speech. "Just look at this dump! Why, some animals live better than we do."

Rod remained silent. He had never heard June talk like that before in their twelve years of marriage.

Rod and June had met one night at a church youth fellowship in a small town in North Dakota. While driving around town, Rod had decided to go to church for the fun of it. He had slipped in through the back door and sat down in a back pew.

Having been the town's high school football star, Rod was well-known; so after the service, a number of people gathered around the unexpected visitor to express their pleasure in seeing him.

"Hey, Rod," called one of the fellows. "We're going to have a pizza party downstairs. Why don't you join us?"

Rod enjoyed being the celebrity of the evening as he answered questions about his football days.

During the latter part of the evening, Rod happened to sit by a pretty blonde girl.

"I remember when you were a sophomore," said Rod. "I assume," he continued with a slight smile, "that you are now a senior."

He noticed the girl blush when he spoke to her.

"I am," responded June. "I'm really looking forward to graduation. I have a scholarship to go to a Bible college."

"Bible college," queried Rod with a puzzled look. "What's that?"

"Well, that is where you study the Bible as well as other subjects."

"I see," Rod replied, pretending he thoroughly understood.

Before leaving the group that night, he shook June's hand and told her how much he had enjoyed talking with her. For the next three Sundays Rod James went to church. He even professed to receive Christ as his Savior in order to strengthen a growing relationship with June. Four weeks after he met June, he asked her for a date.

Her parents, upon June's insistence that Rod was showing spiritual growth and really needed Christian fellowship, gave their approval. Rod was wise enough not to say or do anything on the date that would embarrass June. The relationship continued to grow.

The day after graduation, Rod presented June with an engagement ring. By that time June believed she loved Rod and wanted to become his bride. All thoughts of Bible school had been forgotten. The wedding took place three months later, and it was during their honeymoon that June first saw Rod take a drink. His church attendance was over as far as he was concerned. He was determined to change June as well.

The young bride came home from her honeymoon with a heavy heart. She realized she had fallen into a horrible trap. Weeks stretched into months, and months into years. June stopped going to church and eventually began to drink with their friends. Two years after her first drink, June was declared an alcoholic. Rod lost his job in North Dakota and applied to a lumber company in Alaska. Within four weeks he and June moved to Alaska; however, his drinking habits continued to interfere with his work and he was released.

Not long after Rod lost his job, they lost their home as well and moved into an abandoned shack outside the city. Rod and June James had sunk just about as low as they could go. They went into town regularly and begged money from people to pay for their drinks.

One day there was a knock on the door. Through bleary, blood-shot eyes, June saw a middle-aged man standing before her. He smiled as he spoke.

"I'm Paul Warner. I'm trying to establish a church in town, and I'm calling on people in the community. Could I have a few minutes of your time, please?"

June knew what the man was saying, but her thinking was too fogged to carry on an intelligent conversation with him. "Can you come back another time?" she asked. "My husband is sick."

The visitor nodded and handed her a piece of paper. "I'll leave this with you," he said. "It tells about me and the work that I want to begin. If I can be of any help to you, please let me know."

Now June stirred and picked up the piece of paper given to her the day before by the visitor, inviting them to come to his meetings.

"Rod," she announced, rising to her feet and taking the coffee pot off the top of the stove. "I'm going to do something about the way we've been living."

She poured coffee for both of them. After drinking their coffee, they stretched out on the mattress which lay on the floor. Rod had found the mattress in the town dump the year before. Long after her husband had fallen asleep, June lay quietly with her tears wetting the mattress. She thought of her parents, her Christian upbringing, her marriage to Rod and the horrible, sinful life she had lived since. The next morning she awoke determined to continue where she had left off the night before. She cleaned up the room as best as she could.

"I've had enough too," Rod admitted as he helped her clean up the place. "I've made a mess of our lives. Maybe that missionary can help us, June."

The distraught couple bundled up in what warm clothing they had and within fifteen minutes arrived in town. They found the missionary's house and knocked on the door, shaking with cold and fear. A pretty brunette with a little girl beside her opened the door.

"We've come to see the missionary," said Rod, through chattering teeth.

"Please come in," spoke the woman in her soft voice. "I'll call my husband. He's in the basement making a sign for our meeting place."

The bright, cheery home was like a tonic to Rod and June. In a minute, Paul Warner appeared. He knew by looking at them that they were poor and probably had not had a good warm meal in a long time. They took off their coats and sat down with him in the living room. It took only minutes for Paul to realize that Rod was not saved and that June was a backslidden Christian. With his open Bible before him, Paul had the joy of hearing Rod ask God to forgive him of his sins and to save him. June, too, wept openly as she confessed her sinful past to the Lord, asking for restoration. The missionary couple asked Rod and June to stay with them for lunch, which they gladly accepted.

Before lunch they were taken to the basement where to their surprise they saw a number of large boxes which contained beautiful used and new clothing.

"These are from our supporting churches," explained Paul. "We want you to take what you can use. There is no limit." The two couples loaded their arms with clothing which Rod and June picked out and carried the precious gifts upstairs.

The overwhelming turn of events was almost too much for June. They had been miraculously delivered from a life of alcoholism. After losing nearly everything they had ever owned, they now sat at a table of delicious food with new friends who showed genuine love for them. Behind them on the sofa was a stack of clothing which they so desperately needed. And best of all, Rod was now a Christian.

As Paul gave thanks for the food, June squeezed Rod's hand. She could feel the tears trickle down her face. Rod and June James had already seen a glorious change and were on the threshold of a new beginning.

IT'S YOUR LIFE

Helen tightly gripped the songbook she held in her hands as she nervously waited to sing the second verse of the familiar invitation hymn as a solo. Her legs trembled slightly and beads of perspiration appeared on her forehead. She knew what she would sing was far from the truth in her own life. Nevertheless, at a cue from the choir leader, Helen began in her beautiful soprano voice "All to Jesus I surrender."

Helen was the only child of Tom and Margaret Hart. Committed to the Lord at birth, Helen had accepted Christ as her Savior when she was six years old. She practically grew up in the church, participating in all of the youth activities. Pastor Wood knew that in Helen he always had someone on whom he could count to help in the work.

Helen took her parents by surprise when she announced to them on her sixteenth birthday that she would not be going to Bible college as she had been planning to do.

"I don't want to go to Bible college, Mom. I really would like to go to the community college here in the city."

Her parents could hardly believe they were hearing this from their daughter.

"But, honey," protested Helen's mother, "not only would you get a good education, but you would be taught by Christian teachers and have the opportunity of meeting many Christian young people. Before you make your final decision, why don't you pray about it?"

"I don't need to pray about it, Mom. That's what I'm trying to tell you. I want to go to the community college."

The sound of Helen's voice pierced her parents' hearts like a dagger. She turned and went quickly up the steps to her room, slamming the bedroom door behind her.

"What has happened to our daughter, Margaret?" asked Tom, with a strange look on his face. "She has never talked to us like that before."

"I'm not sure, honey," answered the concerned mother. "I may be wrong, but I have a suspicion that Helen has met a boy attending the community college and that he may not be a Christian."

Thirty minutes later Helen came back down.

"I'm sorry for the way I talked to you and for slamming my bedroom door. I guess I just don't want to be forced into doing things that I don't want to do. I'm sure you understand that."

"Honey, is there something troubling you that you can share with Mom and me?" asked her father. "If there is, maybe we can help you with it."

"There's nothing wrong. I guess I just feel pressured to do things, and after awhile it bothers me."

Even though Helen tried to sound like the Helen that her parents once knew and wanted to hear, a rebellious spirit came through clearly.

"I know you're not going to like this, Mom and Dad, but I'm going to stop helping Mrs. Brown with her Sunday School class. Those kids get on my nerves."

"But, honey," cried her mother, "you're a big help to Mrs. Brown, and she really appreciates all that you're doing."

"She can get someone else to help her," responded Helen "I've been thinking of quitting the choir too."

Before either of her parents could respond to what Helen had said, she turned to the front door to leave the house.

"As long as I'm telling you these things, I might as well inform you that I have changed my style of music. I'm listening now to what some people call Christian rock."

Helen went out to the front porch, stood there a few seconds and then went down the steps to walk out to the street. She turned to see her mother standing in the doorway.

"I'll be right back, Mom. I have to meet one of the kids from church down at the drugstore."

Once around the corner, Helen made her way quickly through a side street to a waiting car in a parking lot.

"Hi, gorgeous," the young man sitting in the car greeted her. Helen climbed in the front seat with him.

"I can't stay long, Eddie. I told Mom and Dad I'd be right back." Eddie Morgan was in his freshman year at the community college.

"Now that's disappointing," he frowned. "I thought maybe we could take in a movie."

"Not tonight, Eddie. I've got Mom and Dad pretty well upset now, and I don't want to do anything more that is going to make it worse for me at home."

"Why don't you leave home?" Eddie asked with a serious tone in his voice. "Look, Helen, you don't think like they do. You've told me that yourself. Why should they force their religion on you?"

Helen saw immediately the damage she had done in living two lives. She knew that having Eddie meant giving up some things that she had known from her childhood days, such as church and her Christian friends.

"Just give me time to work it out, Eddie. That's all I need—just a little time."

"Okay, Babe. It's your life, and you know what you're doing."

Unknown to Eddie, his words had struck deeply into Helen's heart. She realized that it *was* her life—but the only life that she would ever have.

"Well, I've got to go, Eddie. I promised Mom and Dad that I'd be right back, and I'd better keep my promise."

Eddie reached over and pulled Helen close to him. "Well, at least I can have a kiss before you go."

Helen pulled away, opened the door and stepped out onto the parking lot.

"Well, don't go away mad," protested Eddie, half laughing. "What about tomorrow night?"

"We'll see," replied Helen, walking away from the car and heading back home. As she neared the edge of the parking lot, she heard the tires squeal behind her as Eddie sped out onto the street. Helen had identified the problem in her life. If she was to have any peace at all, she had to deal with that problem.

The next two days were relatively quiet for Helen. There had been no contact with Eddie Morgan. Sunday morning she helped Mrs. Brown with her Sunday School class as usual.

Pastor Wood preached a message on dedication and God dealt with Helen throughout the service. She saw clearly the two lives that she had been living. Tears came to her eyes as she glanced down at her mother and father sitting in the second row. The choir was singing the invitational hymn while Pastor Wood stood down front waiting for any who wanted to come forward to indicate a decision made for the Lord.

Helen's beautiful soprano voice captivated the congregation.

"I surrender all. I surrender all. All to Thee, my blessed Savior. I surrender all."

After her solo, Helen stepped out from her position in the choir and made her way down to where Pastor Wood was standing. Simultaneously her mother and father joined her at the front of the auditorium—each with an arm around their daughter.

"I've been living two lives, Pastor Wood," admitted Helen. "I've been dating an unsaved guy. I've been unkind to Mom and Dad too. I need to get my life straightened out."

The understanding pastor listened carefully to Helen.

"Praise the Lord, Helen. God has a job for you to do, young lady. We are convinced that with this kind of dedication, you will enjoy the blessings of doing that job for Him."

That afternoon, Helen wrote to a Christian college requesting an application.

KIDNAPPED FOR GOOD

A blood-curdling scream brought Helen wide-awake.

"What's that?" she cried, feeling for her flashlight under her pillow.

Bill, also awakened by the scream, reached for his flashlight as well.

"There it is again," said Helen. "It sounds like it's in the woods behind the house."

Bill loosened the mosquito net from underneath the mattress and reached over for his slippers on a nearby chair. Slipping into his bathrobe, he made his way to the window and looked out upon the forest.

"I don't see anything," he whispered. "I can't understand why John isn't out of his hut. Surely he must have heard those screams." John was their elderly night watchman, who slept in a small grass hut near the edge of the concession. Making his way to the kerosene lamp on the dresser, Bill struck a match and lit the wick, lighting the entire room. A look at his watch told him it was just a few minutes after 3 a.m.

"Do you have any idea what it is?" asked Helen, slipping into her robe.

"No, I really don't," Bill responded. "Had the sound come from the village, I would understand it, but this came from the forest. No one ever goes into the forest in the middle of the night unless it is absolutely necessary."

By the time Bill was dressed, he noticed the light of a kerosene lantern outside in the backyard. When he opened the door, the night watchman stood there.

"Who screamed, John?" inquired Bill, stepping out into the yard.

"That's the work of Sioni," answered the elderly man.

"You mean, Sioni, the witch doctor?" responded the veteran missionary.

John nodded his head while making a clicking noise in his throat.

"Tell me, John, what has Sioni done? Who was the person who screamed?"

The night watchman hesitated before he answered. "It was Marie. She was kidnapped from the village and is being taken to the Yondo camp for her initiation scars."

"Oh no," cried Helen, who was standing in the doorway. "Not Marie!"

"Yes, Marie, Mrs. Ball," replied John. "We have tried to hide all of the talk that is going around because we did not want you to worry. The witch doctor is determined to make Marie go through the initiation ceremonies and get her tribal scars like the other adults in the tribe."

Marie was the daughter of a national pastor who had died of malaria three years before. He had been carried to the mission station for treatment but was too far gone and had died the next day. After his death, Marie and her mother came to live in the mission village next to the mission station. They felt they could serve the Lord together, helping with classes in the local church. Marie's father, Pastor Mark, had been determined at any cost to protect his daughter from the evil tribal ceremonies. His own life had been threatened a number of times because of his determination not to support the old tribal customs.

"Can't we go and rescue her, John?" asked Bill, sounding extremely frustrated.

"Not now," answered the old African. "We would only bring harm to Marie if we started out now. They are still too close. We have already made plans in case something like this happened, Mr. Ball."

Bill knew the Africans well enough that when one of them spoke as John was speaking, they had thought out their plans and knew exactly what they were going to do.

"Four of our men will leave the village just before the sun comes up. If all goes well, we will have Marie back here with us by nightfall or before the following morning. We know exactly where the Yondo camp is located and all the paths that lead to it."

"But once they reach the camp, they may cut her body immediately," said Bill.

"They won't ever reach the camp," responded John, with authority and certainty in his voice. "We know their plans quite well, and we know just where we will ambush them and take Marie."

* * * *

"Please let me go," pleaded Marie to her captors. "I belong to God. He owns my body. It is His, and I don't want to dishonor it with tribal scars."

"We have our orders," growled one of the men. "Our instructions are to deliver you to Sioni. He can do with you as he pleases."

The men released their hold on Marie but made her walk between them. Now and then they stopped to listen to see if they were being followed.

"Jesus loves you both," said Marie, unashamed to speak out for God. "He died for you and paid the penalty for all your sin. He will forgive you for what you are doing right now."

The two men stood in astonishment as they listened to the young woman speaking things they had never heard before.

"My father was one who lived a very evil life. He, too, helped the witch doctor like you men are doing. One day, he heard God's Word spoken by a missionary. The word struck hard at his heart. He finally asked Jesus to come into his heart and make him a child of God. He then met my mother and they went to Bible school where he trained to be a pastor."

The men sat down with Marie to listen to her story.

"One day he caught the fever and died. God took my father home to Heaven. I miss him, but one day I will see him in Heaven. That is the wonderful place that Jesus has prepared for those who have accepted Him into their hearts."

The men asked Marie if God could become their Father like He was her Father.

"Yes, you both can know God as your Father," she answered with excitement.

Within minutes, the men both prayed, asking God to forgive them of their sins and save them.

"We can't go on with you," declared one of the men. "We must take you back to your village. You belong there with your mother."

The three turned to retrace their steps to the mission village.

* * * *

Bill glanced at his wristwatch. It was 10:15 p.m., past bedtime for him and Helen. They had thought perhaps some good news would arrive before they retired for the night. The kerosene lamp on the stand before them became dimmer by the minute.

"I should have filled the lamp today," spoke Helen. "I didn't realize it was so low on—"

She was interrupted by someone clapping his hands in the backyard.

"I wonder who that is," Bill said, picking up his flashlight and heading for the back door. He opened it to find Marie and her mother along with about twenty men standing before him.

"Here she is, Mr. Ball," announced John, smiling. "We didn't have to bring her back. The men who took her did. God worked a miracle for Marie."

Helen slipped by Bill and put her arms around the young African woman.

"Hello Mr. and Mrs. Ball," spoke Marie happily. "I want you to meet Likongo and Zcme."

The two men moved to the front of the others. While they stood there smiling, Marie told what had taken place after she had been kidnapped.

"The four men from our village were ready to fight my new friends when they met us on the path. Once I told them that Likongo and Zeme were their brothers in the Lord, they shook hands and hugged each other."

Marie paused a moment then continued,"Isn't it wonderful the way this all worked out? I'm glad I was kidnapped. Just think, if I wasn't taken, then Likongo and Zeme would not know Jesus as their Savior tonight."

The sound of tongues clicking could be heard throughout the group. They knew they had witnessed a miracle of God.

A GOD OF MIRACLES

Pastor Woods gazed over the congregation as he reported the need for housing for Dr. Peter Andrews, a veteran missionary doctor from Africa. With the annual missionary conference just one week away, the family who was to keep one of three missionaries had withdrawn their invitation because two of their children were ill.

"I don't know Dr. Andrews personally," the pastor stated, "but I have read several of his books, and I'm sure he would be an interesting houseguest and a blessing in your home." The pastor hesitated for a moment and then continued, "I'm wondering if there are any volunteers?"

Almost before Pastor Woods stopped speaking, one of the women in the church raised her hand. "Thank you, Mrs. Mason. I'll give you the necessary details regarding Dr. Andrews after the service."

The church family was surprised that Maureen Mason offered to keep Dr. Andrews. Her husband, a medical doctor, was noted as an outspoken atheist. He bitterly opposed anything that had to do with God and the church.

The Masons had two teenage children, Tom and Lorie. They were forbidden by their father to attend church anywhere. Three years before, when Maureen had been led to Christ by one of the ladies at the church, her husband threatened to divorce her but then reconsidered. He told her that she could go to church, but he did not want her to bother him or the children with her "fanatic beliefs."

Immediately after the service, Pastor Woods spoke with Mrs. Mason.

"Maureen, please understand me. I know the situation in your home. If you want to change your mind about having Dr. Andrews come and stay with you folks, I will understand."

"Pastor Woods," responded Maureen, "I feel in my heart that God has given me an opportunity to do something for Him. I don't know what Harry will say when I tell him, but I'm sure the Lord will handle it for me."

As Maureen drove into their driveway, she noticed Harry lifting his golf bag out of the trunk of his car.

"Where are the children?" asked Maureen, getting out of her car.

"Oh, they're inside watching a movie. I told them I would take them swimming this afternoon over at the lake."

Even though Harry despised his wife's beliefs, he was helpful to her around the house. While both of them were preparing the noon meal, Maureen decided that she would tell Harry about her invitation to keep Dr. Andrews.

"You did what!" said Harry, straightening up with his hands on his hips.

"I told Pastor Woods that we would keep Dr. Andrews during our missionary conference."

"Why would you do a thing like that?" questioned Harry, his face flushed with anger.

"It was an emergency, Harry," spoke Maureen in her soft voice. "The other family that was going to keep him had to withdraw their invitation because of illness."

"How long is he going to stay?" asked Harry, somewhat less irritated because of Maureen's explanation.

"He will arrive Saturday evening and leave Thursday morning."

Harry was mowing the lawn when Dr. Peter Andrews pulled into the driveway Saturday afternoon. He sized up their visitor quickly, noting he was a pleasant-looking, rather tall man with a tinge of gray hair at the temples. The two men shook hands. Harry offered to help their visitor into the house with his suitcases. As soon as the trunk lid was opened, Harry spotted the long spearheads and a rolled python skin.

"Well, what have we here?" said Harry.

"Oh, I carry these things with me," said Dr. Andrews. "You being in the medical profession, I'm sure I have some slides that would be of interest to you."

For some reason Harry felt comfortable with Peter Andrews. That night at the evening meal, the Mason family sat spellbound as the veteran missionary doctor shared some of this experiences with them. After the meal, Harry and Peter went into the front room to talk. Never before in his profession had Harry Mason had the opportunity to get first-hand information on areas about which he had only read in medical books.

"I know you are tired from traveling," said Harry. "But I'm wondering if you could show a few slides tonight?"

"Great," responded Peter. "I have lots of them with me, and what we don't show here I will show you during the missionary conference."

"Well, uh, yes, of course," answered Harry hesitantly. "I'll get the screen. We can set it up right here."

Maureen Mason, working in the kitchen, had heard the entire conversation and was quietly praying that God would work in her husband's heart. Within ten minutes, the two medical doctors sat viewing pictures of Peter's work in Africa.

"Those are absolutely fantastic!" exclaimed Harry. "The fellows at the hospital would love to see pictures like this."

"Well, this is what I work with every day," returned Peter. "I'm sure that you would really be challenged with some of the cases that come to me at the mission hospital."

The two men talked until midnight. "This has been

some evening," said Harry, looking over at Maureen, who had quietly joined them.

"By the way, Maureen, where is that red and gray tie that Tom bought me for Christmas? I want to wear it to church tomorrow."

A thrill of excitement rippled through Maureen's body.

"I'll go look for it," she offered, nearly overwhelmed with all that was happening.

Before he went to bed, Harry Mason informed Tom and Lorie that they were to get dress clothes ready to go to church in the morning. They both looked rather strangely at their father sand then turned to do what he had asked them.

Pastor Woods, who knew Dr. Mason on a professional basis, greeted him, as well as Tom and Lorie, warmly. Maureen Mason looked happier than she had for the past three years.

Harry's eyes were glued on the missionary doctor as he spoke. Peter closed his Bible and looked out over the congregation. "I have never been in this church before. I don't know any of you outside the Mason family, whom I met only yesterday, and the pastor and his wife, whom I met this morning. But, dear friends, isn't it amazing that even though we have never met before, because of our faith in Jesus Christ, we have that common bond between us? It is a miracle of God. Friend, if you are here this morning and you don't know the joy of God's salvation provided through the death of His dear Son, Jesus Christ, I personally invite you today to acknowledge your lost condition and trust Him to save you."

Harry reached over and took Maureen by the hand. He bowed his head and squeezed his eyes shut to hold back the tears. At the first note of the invitation hymn, the entire Mason family rose to their feet and went forward to clasp the hands of Pastor Woods and Peter Andrews. That morning, Dr. Harry Mason and his two teenage children accepted Christ as their Savior.

Before the conference ended, Tom and Lorie had committed themselves to go to Bible college, and Harry had arranged with Peter to go to Africa for six weeks the following summer to help in the hospital work. Maureen Mason, a faithful testimony for God and a woman sensitive to the leading of the Holy Spirit, rejoiced in the fact that God had heard and answered her prayers in a miraculous way.

"Truly," she told Pastor Woods, "He is a God of miracles."

TRUSTING GOD FOR THE FUTURE

Jim Oakley was training to be a policeman when he met Janet Vogel in the hospital where she worked. It was love at first sight.

Their first date was a double date with some friends of Janet's who invited her and Jim to go with them to a meeting in the city's civic auditorium. Little did Jim and Janet realize the events of that evening would change their lives. As they walked into the huge auditorium, they noticed many of the people were carrying Bibles.

"I've never seen so many Bibles in my life," whispered Jim. "What kind of meeting is this anyway?"

Janet pressed a finger against her lips. She didn't want her friends to hear Jim.

The meeting began with singing hymns which were familiar even to Jim and Janet, although neither of them attended church. The music captured their attention as one group after another sang.

Jim paid special attention when a well-known major league baseball player walked to the microphone and told how he had become a Christian and what Christ meant to him.

The speaker for the evening was a former gangster from Philadelphia. He quoted many Bible verses as he spoke. Listening to him, the audience was moved to laughter and tears. Jim and Janet had never heard anything like it. He told how he had been born and raised in a so-called religious home.

"I was religious," he said, "but religiously blind to the truth of God's Word. You can know there is a God. You can even believe that there is a Heaven and a hell, but unless you acknowledge your sinful condition and receive Christ as your Savior, you are doomed and lost forever."

Jim felt uneasy as he listened to the message. When the service came to a close, the choir on the platform sang an invitation song while the speaker invited those without Christ to come forward. Without hesitation, Janet stood up and headed for the aisle. Jim immediately followed. That night, Jim Oakley and Janet Vogel were born again.

They began attending Calvary Baptist Church, which was near the hospital where Janet worked. Six months later, Jim asked Janet to marry him, and eight months after their engagement they were married.

During a missionary conference in their church, the young couple yielded their lives to the Lord for missionary service. After counseling with their pastor, they applied to a Bible college. That fall, Jim and Janet were students in college, majoring in Bible and missions. During their second year of college, God spoke to their hearts about the country of Brazil. Once again, they yielded their lives according to the leading of the Holy Spirit.

The young couple devoted themselves to their studies and enjoyed the many friends the Lord brought into their lives. The four years of college passed quickly for them, and their excitement grew as they applied to a mission board for service in Brazil.

"God bless you, Jim and Janet," spoke the college president as he handed them their graduation certificates. Within two months Jim and Janet appeared before the mission board for doctrinal examination. Once again God proved His faithfulness to them as He helped them respond to the questions satisfactorily.

"I can hardly believe all the wonderful things that God has done for us," spoke Janet to the deputation administrator of the mission. "Jim and I are really excited about sharing our call and burden for Brazil with the churches."

As the young couple became involved in their deputation ministry, God opened doors and touched hearts. Within twelve months, they had raised their required monthly support and were given approval by the mission board to begin their passport and visa applications. Many from their home church arrived at the airport to bid farewell to Jim and Janet as they headed for the mission field.

"Father," prayed their pastor at the airport, "we are following Your command as we send these dear ones forth. We commit them once again into Your care and pray that You will use them to win many to Jesus Christ."

* * * *

"Welcome to Brazil," one of the missionaries greeted Jim and Janet at the airport. "We all have been looking forward to meeting you."

The energetic couple began their language study. To the pleasant surprise of all, they did better than average. Brazilians and missionary coworkers alike fell in love with Jim and Janet. It hardly seemed that they had begun their work when their four-year term was over. It was time to return to the States for furlough.

Pastor Brown, along with a group of people from the church, met them at the airport. "Welcome home," he said, hugging Jim and Janet. "We have prayed for you every day since you left us."

"We have something to express the love of your church for you. We've been doing some planning while you were away from us." As he spoke some of the congregation chuckled. He then called the chairman of the deacons, Bill Nichols, to come forward. Jim and Janet felt a bit nervous, not knowing what to expect.

"We love you, Jim and Janet, and what I am about to

say doesn't really begin to express our love for you. Our Calvary Baptist Church family has purchased a new car for you, and I'm happy to present you with the keys. Now before you drive away in it," he said with a slight grin and a chuckle, "I want to give you this envelope."

Jim's hand shook with excitement as he took the envelope from the deacon. He opened it to find a check for $1,000 and a note informing them that they had a three week's vacation in Hawaii paid for by the church.

"Thank you," whispered Jim, hardly able to speak. "Thank you," repeated Janet, wiping the tears from her eyes.

That week Jim and Janet flew to Hawaii to enjoy the vacation their church family had given to them. While reading the Bible with Janet one morning in their hotel room prior to their planned day's activities, Jim looked up with a strange look on his face. He put his hand to his head and whispered, "Janet, I . . .," and fell forward on the table. Jim, without any notice, was called home to Heaven.

Four days later, Janet sat in the front pew of Calvary Baptist Church. Some fifteen feet away was the coffin holding the body of her beloved husband. The events of the past several days were almost overwhelming to the young widow.

"Father," she prayed silently, "I don't understand why all of this has happened. I do know that You love me and want Your best for me. You have chosen to take Jim home. Please help me to be faithful to You. Help me to carry on the work that You have called me to do."

Janet Oakley had passed another milestone in her young life and was trusting God for the future.

THE STRANGER

The talking drums beat out the message loudly and clearly. The people in the villages within hearing distance stopped whatever they were doing to listen.

"All eligible youth must go to the initiation camp tomorrow. Anyone violating this command will be punished."

The sound of the drums echoed throughout the nearby forests. In village after village the drummers picked up the message of the area's head witch doctor to transmit it to other villages. The witch doctor wanted to be sure that no one would miss hearing the important tribal order.

Mark stood motionless, listening to the dreaded message, knowing that he was one of the teenagers commanded to participate in the tribal ceremonies. He had been a Christian for two years but managed to escape the ceremonies the year before due to his small size. Now, the only way he could avoid them was to go into hiding somewhere.

He walked slowly over to his father, who sat carving a handle for a garden hoe. The serious look on his face showed that he was deep in thought.

"What can I do, Father?" asked Mark softly. "I can't let them give me those scars. My body belongs to God."

Mark's father, Toro, nodded his head in agreement. A clicking sound came from his throat.

The young African continued speaking quietly to his father. "Then there's the blood sacrifices I would be forced to make. I love Jesus, Father. I can't do that to Him!"

"You have grown strong in the faith, Mark," spoke Toro without looking up at his son. "I know you are not afraid of the knife cuts over your body or even the beatings which you would go through."

"You're right, Father," responded Mark. How thankful he was for a father who was a Christian and loved God. Mark's mother had died three years before when she was gored by a wounded cape buffalo while working in her garden.

"Tonight I'm leaving the village," announced Mark in a determined voice. "If I stay here, they will force me to go. I will not make those sacrifices or choose a god that I'm supposed to serve the rest of my life."

Again, a clicking sound came from Toro's throat indicating agreement with his son. He knew that the separation could possibly be for years, as it would be necessary for Mark to leave the tribe's territory. He might even have to go into a neighboring country.

Toro sat striking the hoe handle with a small hatchet. His heart was heavy, knowing there was no choice but for Mark to leave. The possibility of a compromise did not even exist in the minds of either father or son. Mark knew that if he gave in and went to the jungle camp, he would be able to stay in the tribe. Without his scars, however, he would never be looked upon as an adult or accepted by the tribe.

That night Toro helped his son pack his small multicolored plywood suitcase. In the dim light of the small kerosene lantern, Mark could see the tears running down his father's face. Very few words were spoken between the two, who knew what had to be done and were determined to do it.

The flame in the small lantern was blown out just after midnight. Toro, who had just prayed, committing his son to the Lord, slowly opened the door. Making sure the village was clear, he took Mark by the arm and guided him out into the darkness. In seconds, Mark disappeared into the night leaving his grieving father behind.

The next morning, the news spread quickly that Mark had left the village so he would not have to go to the tribal ceremonies. The local witch doctor came to see Toro to ask where Mark was hiding.

"I don't know," replied the African repeatedly. "I have no idea where he went."

Each day brought with it long, lonely hours for Toro. He missed his beloved son more than words could describe. Five days had gone by when he received the first news of Mark. He was sweeping in front of his hut when a tall, middle-aged man approached him.

"Is your name Toro?" asked the stranger, keeping his voice low so others could not hear him speak.

"Yes, I'm Toro."

"Are you the father of Mark?"

"Mark is my son. Why do you ask these questions?"

"I am a friend," the visitor responded. "I talked to your son two days ago. He was riding on the top of a loaded truck that was headed out of the country. They had stopped in a village near the border to buy food. I noticed your son did not have his tribal scars so I asked him why. I told him that I was a friend and that I knew his God."

Toro clicked his tongue while nodding his head. "Please go on."

"Mark then told me why he was fleeing the country. I bought him some food and gave him some money. You have a good son, Toro. You don't have to worry about him getting into trouble."

Toro invited the stranger to stay with him for the night. He knew that God had answered his prayers and sent him the news concerning Mark.

That night while Toro and his guest slept, someone set fire to the grass roof of his hut. Within seconds, it was a roaring inferno. The visitor awoke and shouted to Toro.

"Fire! Wake up, Toro. Your house is on fire!"

The man then dashed through the flames which

blocked the doorway. He turned just in time to see the roof collapse. Toro was trapped inside.

The next day, the village chief, learning that the stranger was the one who knew Toro's God, asked him to say something at Toro's funeral. The entire village turned out to hear what he had to say.

"You don't know me," he began. "Toro didn't know me either until yesterday afternoon when I walked into your village. We knew immediately that we had something in common. We love and serve the same God."

Several nodded their heads as the visitor spoke.

"Toro had a very heavy heart. He was grieving the absence of his only son, Mark, who fled so he wouldn't be forced to go against the will of his God."

The clicking of tongues could be heard throughout the crowd. The stranger continued.

"Someone murdered Toro simply because he believed in Jesus and stood up for what he believed. This is only the remains of his shell before us wrapped in that cloth. The real Toro is in Heaven where there is no evil and no suffering. God has prepared a place for Toro where he can live forever."

Some of the villagers began to get restless. Seeing this, the speaker went on.

"How many of you are sure of living forever in God's village when you die?"

"You sound like Toro," said the village chief. "We need to hear those good words again. Please tell us. Toro had tried to talk to us many times, but we would not listen. Now our ears are open to hear."

The stranger spoke a few minutes more and then asked those who would like to receive Jesus to step forward. Ten of the villagers including the chief came forward. The man spoke and prayed with them.

A strange silence fell upon the village. The only sounds that could be heard were made by the two men shoveling dirt into the open grave. The chief knew that Toro's God was now his God—a God Who sent a stranger to give them the message of life.

THE BACKYARD TIRE SWING

The loud hissing sound and sudden lurch of the car caused Dave to pull over to the side of the road.

"What's wrong, Daddy?" called ten-year-old Janet from the back seat. "What's that noise?"

"Oh no," groaned Dave as he got out of the car and looked at the left back tire. "Now what are we going to do? That was our spare."

Five miles back Dave had run over a piece of metal in the road, cutting the other tire so badly that it could not be repaired.

"How far back was that last house that we saw?" asked Marilyn, squinting her eyes in the sunlight shining through the windshield.

"It must be at least two miles," answered Dave. To his surprise, he found another piece of steel the same size as the one that had destroyed the first tire.

"It must be that a truck hauling these scraps of steel passed by here, dropping the pieces of steel on the road."

"Well, the first thing we're going to do," announced Dave, crawling back into the car, "is to ask the Lord to help us get a tire somewhere."

The little family bowed their heads while Dave asked God to lead them to where they could get a tire to fit the car. He got back out of the car, opened the trunk and took out the jack in order to examine the tire.

Dave soon had the wheel off the ground and rotated it to assess the damage. There was no hope that the tire could be repaired.

"What are we going to do, Daddy" asked Janet. "Is somebody going to come and help us?"

"I hope so, honey," responded her father. "Jesus knows all about it, and He will help us somehow."

A car came by and stopped. Sitting behind the wheel was a young woman, who asked with a pleasant smile, "Can I help you?"

"Perhaps you can," answered Dave. "Within five miles we have destroyed two tires from pieces of steel that were on the road."

"You're not alone," returned the young lady. "There have been a lot of cars with flat tires along here since those trucks started hauling scraps of steel. Please get in. I'll do what I can to help you."

"Do you know of a place where we can purchase tires?" asked Dave.

"Well, the nearest place is about twenty miles away. My brother, however, has many different tires in our garage. We live about three miles back down the road."

"Then that must have been your house we passed," spoke Dave.

"Yes, that's where I live," spoke the girl. Within minutes she drove into the driveway. Her twin brother Billy came out of the garage when he saw her.

"Billy," she called, "these people need a tire for their car. Do you have one around that they can have?"

"Why don't you take the lady and the little girl into the house, Karen? Her husband and I can go and get the wheel off the car and bring it back here. I might have a tire to fit it."

"We are Dave and Marilyn Green," spoke Dave. "Our daughter's name is Janet."

"Nice to meet you, Mr. Green," said Billy, smiling.

Within twenty minutes Dave and Billy were back at the garage. "Boy, I don't know," said Billy as he looked over a stack of used tires. "I thought I might have something here that we could put on your car. I used to have a car that took those size tires."

He opened a drawer and pulled out an inner tube. "Well, what do you know? We at least have a tube that would fit the tire. Now, if we could only find the tire."

Billy continued to search about the garage.

"Well, I'm sorry, Mr. Green. I thought I had a tire here, but I don't."

"Look, Daddy, I'm swinging," called Janet from the backyard. Billy's sister Karen was pushing Janet on a tire hung by a rope from the limb of a tree.

"Hey, there it is," cried Billy excitedly. "That's the tire I've been looking for. I forgot I made a swing for our little niece who comes to visit us now and then."

The two men walked over to the swing. Dave saw that the tire still had good tread on it. "That tire looks like it is practically brand new."

"Well, not quite, Mr. Green, but it does have a lot of wear in it yet."

Karen helped Janet out of the tire, which Billy quickly untied and took to the garage. Within a short time he had the tire and tube on the rim. The two men put the wheel in the trunk of Karen's car and headed off for the disabled vehicle.

"How much do I owe you?" asked Dave, looking over at Billy.

"You don't owe me anything, Mr. Green. That tire was only being used for a swing and the inner tube—well, to tell you the truth, I really had forgotten about that. I'm just glad to help you."

"Well, thank you, Billy," responded Dave, "and thank the Lord for directing us to you."

Billy looked at Dave rather strangely after hearing his remark.

"What do you mean by that?" asked Billy.

"Well, you see," replied Dave, "the three of us are Christians. We have accepted Christ as our Savior, and we talk to the Lord about most everything."

"You mean to say that you told God about your flat tire?"

"Oh yes," said Dave. "In fact, as soon as I saw what happened, we asked the Lord right there in the car to lead us to a place where we could get a tire."

"And you believe that God hears you when you ask Him for things like that?" questioned Billy with a serious look on his face.

"He sure does," returned Dave, smiling. "He knows all about us. He loves us and watches over us."

"Boy, you really know God, don't you?" asked Billy.

"He's our Heavenly Father," continued Dave, "and we love Him with all our hearts."

The men arrived at the car and soon had the wheel on. Dave followed Billy back to the farm. When they got out of the car, Karen and her parents, along with Marilyn and Janet, came out of the house.

Before any of the adults could say anything, little Janet spoke. "Daddy, Jesus did hear us, didn't He? He helped us to get a tire."

"That's right, honey. Jesus did hear us."

Billy, Karen and their parents stood silent, surprised to hear a little girl talk like that about Jesus.

"Thank you, Karen, I had a nice time," said Janet.

Karen's eyes moistened with tears as she put her arms around the little girl.

"You're welcome, honey," she whispered, patting Janet's shoulder.

"If you folks are in no great hurry," Karen's mother offered, "we would love to have you stay for dinner."

"Why don't you?" inquired Billy. "In fact, we even have a couple of spare bedrooms. Why don't you stay with us for dinner and overnight, too?"

Dave looked at Marilyn. "What do you want to do, honey?"

"Well, it is getting rather late, and we still have to look for a motel."

"That does it. There isn't a motel within fifty miles of here, so why don't you just spend the night with us?" insisted Billy.

"Can we do that, Mommy?" asked Janet, holding Karen's hand.

Dave and Marilyn looked at each other and smiled. "If you're sure that we won't be a burden to you," Dave responded.

"Of course not," spoke Karen's father. "Let's get your things from the car and go in. We really haven't gotten to know each other yet. Besides, we want to hear more about Janet's talk with Jesus."

Dave smiled at Marilyn upon hearing the remark.

As they all walked into the house, Dave looked over at the left rear tire and then glanced at the rope dangling from the tree limb in the backyard.

"Who would have ever thought," he said to Marilyn, "that a tire swing would be God's answer to our prayers?"

Dave and Marilyn Green knew that they were going to have a pleasant evening with their newly-made friends, sharing with them about the Lord.

FOR MY GOOD

Lynn Wood stirred and opened her eyes. "Where am I?"

Barbara Wood moved quickly to the bedside of her sixteen-year-old daughter. Lynn had been flirting with death for the past five days as she lay unconscious at Lakeside Hospital.

The excited mother reached out and touched her daughter's face. "You're in the hospital, honey; but don't worry, the doctors and nurses are taking very good care of you."

"What happened, Mom?"

A nurse entered the room to check Lynn's chart. Her face beamed as she heard Lynn speaking to her mother.

"Well, good morning, Lynn. I'm Betty." The nurse's face glowed with joy at seeing her patient conscious. After a short conversation with Lynn's mother, the nurse went to page Lynn's doctor.

Lynn Wood was the youngest of three children. Her older brother and sister, like Lynn, had accepted Christ as their Savior at an early age. The entire Wood family was very active at church.

During her high school years, unknown to her parents, Lynn became involved in drugs. This led to occasional drinking of alcoholic beverages and secretly dating unsaved men. Before leaving for school one day, Lynn asked her mother if she would mend a dress which had a small tear in it. Taking the dress out of the closet, Lynn's mother noticed a packet of matches on the floor. When she picked them up, she saw advertised a saloon in a nearby town. That afternoon, when Lynn arrived home, her mother questioned her about the book of matches.

"I have no idea how they got there," lied Lynn, with a sharpness to her voice. "I hope, Mom, that you don't think that I go to places like that."

Lynn sounded convincing, but somehow the conversation did not take away the seed of doubt that was planted in her mother's heart. Barbara Wood had noticed some changes taking place in Lynn's life before the discovery of the matches. Her attitude toward her family was not what it should have been. A week after Lynn's mother discovered the packet of matches, she thought she smelled alcohol on Lynn's breath when she kissed her goodnight.

Barbara Wood, for the past three years, had been a widow. Her husband had collided with a truck in a snowstorm. He was taken to the hospital unconscious and remained in that condition until he died a day later.

"Lynn," spoke her mother, "is there something I need to know? Your dad and I committed you children to the Lord when you were born. We made a promise to Him that our home would always be a home where He would be honored. Honey, you know that I don't want to mistrust you, but when you kissed me last night before going up to bed, I thought I smelled alcohol on your breath."

"Mom, will you get off my back?" shouted Lynn. "I've got my own life to live. Just give me a break and let me live it."

The words pierced Barbara Wood's heart like a sword. After Lynn left the house, her mother retreated to the bedroom and knelt, asking God to intervene in Lynn's life and restore her to Himself.

It was the day before the high school prom. Lynn's date was one of the unsaved fellows in her class. "I don't want to interfere in your life, honey, but I don't believe that it pleases the Lord for you to date men who are not Christians," said her mother.

"Bud's just as much a Christian as I am, Mom, even though he may not think the way you do. Besides, being a Christian isn't everything."

Lynn threw her hairbrush down on the floor and went into the next room.

"Dear Father," whispered the burdened mother, "please, somehow bring Lynn back into fellowship with Yourself."

The next night, Lynn's date drove his car into the Woods' driveway and blew the horn. "See ya later, Mom," said Lynn as she closed the front door.

* * * *

"Mrs. Wood?" spoke the voice on the other end of the line. "This is Lakeside Hospital calling." A chill rippled through Barbara's body. Fear gripped her heart as she answered. "Yes, this is Barbara Wood."

The nurse told her a car containing six high school students, three men and three women, had collided with a tractor-trailer truck, killing four of the students and seriously injuring the other two. Lynn and her girlfriend were the survivors of the accident.

Barbara immediately called Pastor James. Her other two children were away at Bible college. "Do you want me to come and get you, Barbara, or can you drive your car?"

"I can drive the car, Pastor," responded the worried mother. "I just thought you should know as soon as possible."

At the hospital, Barbara found it very difficult to look upon her unconscious daughter on the brink of death. For five days she sat at Lynn's bedside praying that God would spare her life. Now, on the sixth day, Lynn had returned to consciousness.

Dr. Brown walked into the room. "Well, my patient has finally decided to wake up and talk to us." A broad smile was on his face.

A few minutes later, as Lynn's thinking continued to improve, she realized that she was in a body cast.

"I can't move my legs," she said anxiously. "What's wrong with me?"

"We really don't know yet, Lynn, but you can be sure that we're going to do everything we can to help you get well."

Hours became days, and days, weeks. Lynn Wood realized that unless God performed a miracle, she would never walk again.

It was a happy day when Lynn was wheeled into her home by her brother, who was given permission from the college to come home for the occasion. Pastor and Mrs. James stood in the front room as Lynn was pushed through the doorway.

"Welcome home, Lynn," Mrs. James greeted her, brushing back a tear as she spoke. Once inside the house, Barbara Wood asked Pastor James to thank God for sparing Lynn's life and bringing her back home.

"Mom, before pastor prays, can I say something?"

Everyone stood in silence as Lynn spoke from her wheelchair.

"God has taught me a lesson," she informed them, dabbing at her eyes as she spoke.

"The way I was going, Mom, my life would have been a catastrophe. I believe what happened to me was for my good, and that God really did me a favor. I've done a lot of thinking in the hospital, and even if I don't walk the rest of my life, I will always thank the Lord for what He allowed to happen to me. Living for God and using my time and talents for Him is more important than anything."

Lynn finished speaking. She bowed her head, waiting for Pastor James to pray.

TARA'S LOVE

Footsteps were approaching quickly. Polly looked out the kitchen window and caught a glimpse of Joel's back as he disappeared around the corner of the building.

"Polly!" he called. "I have good news."

Before Polly could answer, her excited husband burst into the kitchen, his face beaming. He reached out and took her hand.

"The Bibles are here! I saw a transport truck in town and spotted some cases with our name on them. It's our shipment of Bibles."

The shipment of Bibles had been sent from England nearly six months earlier. When they hadn't arrived in the usual two to three months' time, they were feared lost. A tracer put on the shipment revealed that they had not been unloaded in Douala, the seaport in the Cameroons, but mistakenly had been sent to South Africa.

"Wait until our Christians hear about them," continued Joel. "Many of them have been saving their money for a long time to buy a Bible."

"I'm glad that we are able to subsidize the cost at least a little," spoke Polly. "Our people would have a difficult time paying the full price for them."

Joel motioned toward the door. "Let's go outside and wait for the truck in the driveway. It should be coming along any time now."

The truck's motor was music to the missionaries' ears. Its precious cargo represented many years of diligent work by both missionaries and Christian nationals. For months the Christians had been praying for the safe arrival of the Bibles. Now the moment had arrived.

"There it is, Joel!" shouted Polly, half laughing and half crying.

The large truck turned the corner and headed down the long, sandy driveway. Running close behind the truck were the children from the nearby village where many of the church members lived. As they ran, they shouted, sang and clapped their hands.

Joel grinned. "They know what's in those cases."

Men and women seemed to appear from nowhere. As the truck came to a halt, a crowd had already gathered around the missionary couple.

In fifteen minutes the boxes were unloaded and carried into the garage.

"Be sure you put bricks under those boxes," called Joel to the station workmen. "I don't want termites feeding on those Bibles."

Polly gave the driver a big cup of strong black coffee and several sandwiches. He sat on one of the boxes while he ate. Several small children stood close by, wanting to be near the man who could command such a big truck.

"Can we see a Bible, Mr. Hall?" asked one of the Sunday School teachers. "We have waited a long time for this moment."

Joel smiled and picked up a hammer. He took the metal cutting shears off the nail where they hung on the tool board. With two snaps of the shears he cut the metal bands around the box. In minutes he pried open the top of the box and pulled back the protective packing paper.

Every eye was on Joel as he reached into the box and removed a large black Bible. The clicking of tongues was heard throughout the group of believers. Several hummed to show their delight.

"Here it is, my dear brothers and sisters," spoke the

missionary, his voice showing emotion. "This is God's Word in your language. Now you can read it too."

The precious Book was passed around. All wanted to hold the first Bible printed in their language.

"When can we buy them, Mr. Hall?" asked one of the men. "Can we go get our money now?"

"You may all receive your copies tomorrow morning," responded Joel. "I want to get a count first and check out the shipment."

Sitting nearby on the ground was Tara, one of the first believers in the area. Tara had been crippled from birth and had to walk on his hands and knees. He sat gazing at the Bible in Joel's hands.

"I'll be here in the morning, Mr. Hall," announced Tara. "I don't have the money to buy a Bible, but I want to see the joy of my brothers and sisters when they buy their Bibles."

The people turned to look at Tara. They knew that he barely had money on which to live and certainly had no extra money for a Bible.

That evening Joel and Polly sat at the dining room table talking about the Bibles. "Let's give Tara a Bible, honey," suggested Polly. "He doesn't have the money to buy one."

"We will," answered Joel. "When he comes in the morning, I'll surprise him by giving him one."

Before the Hall's alarm went off at five the next morning, the believers had already begun gathering in front of the garage. In thirty minutes Joel and Polly were out with the African Christians. Polly kept looking around for Tara, but he was nowhere in sight.

Joel began handing out the Bibles as the people passed by the boxes. One of the older Christians who never had learned to read nevertheless had her money tied tightly in a cloth. Each one squeezed his Bible as he walked away. Some wept openly for joy.

The crowd suddenly became silent. Every head turned to the path which led to the village. There, making his way down the path, was Tara, walking on his calloused knees and hands. Held tightly in his mouth was a big white rooster. Everyone knew the rooster was Tara's prized possession and the most valuable thing he owned.

Joel and Polly were stunned. They had never witnessed anything quite like this. The elderly Christian made his way through the crowd to the missionaries. Joel reached down and took the rooster from Tara's mouth.

"It's yours, Mr. Hall. I don't have money to buy a Bible. I . . . I thought maybe you would take my rooster for payment."

Tears welled up in Joel's eyes. He tried to talk but found it difficult.

"Thank you, Tara, but you may keep your rooster. Mrs. Hall and I decided last night to give you a Bible."

Joel reached into the box and lifted out a Bible. He motioned for one of the children to come and take it for Tara. Many of the Christians wept as they saw Tara reach up with his calloused hand to shake Joel's hand. With rooster and Bible under his arms, the young lad headed back to the village with Tara.

Polly wiped the tears from her face as she stood watching the elderly man and the young boy go down the path. She turned to Joel.

"I'll never forget this scene, Joel."

"Neither will I, honey. Tara was willing to give the best he had to receive a Bible. I've asked the Lord to help me love and appreciate His Word more than I have in the past. Tara can be a good example for all of us."

"Yes, he can," spoke Polly. "He truly loves God's Word."

THE SEVENTH HOLE

Nice shot," called Ed Jones, as Sam drove the ball two hundred yards straight down the fairway. "Shooting like that, you should be on the green in one more swing."

Sam West, who had just celebrated his sixty-ninth birthday, bent over and picked up his tee which was still in place. "Well, that's my shot for the day," he said, laughing. "I don't get many of those out of my clubs anymore."

Sam, Ed Jones and Phil Thompson had played golf together for years. All three men were presently serving in some capacity in their local church. They loved the Lord and did not hesitate to tell others about Him.

"Well, that's par," Sam announced as he picked his ball out of the cup. "If I could do that on every hole, I might not be retired."

"You mean you'd be a professional golfer?" quipped Phil, patting Sam on the back.

"You never know," spoke up Ed. "We might have a budding professional golfer in our midst." The three friends not only enjoyed their game of golf, but more importantly they also enjoyed the fellowship with each other. Sam played exceptional golf for the first six holes, hitting par in three of them.

"Well, this is the long one," spoke Sam, pointing out toward a clump of pines in the distance. "If I could just hit one over those pines, I'd be on the green in one." "You're right, Sam," agreed Phil. "It's too bad we have to go the long way around, but I've never seen anybody take the shortcut and get away with it."

"Well, here goes," said Sam, as he bent down to press the tee into the ground. His two friends watched him as he hesitated and then fell forward onto the ground. They both rushed to see what had happened, but it was already too late. Sam West was dead.

While Phil Thompson worked on Sam's body to try to revive him, Ed went for help. The doctor later said that Sam was probably gone by the time he hit the ground.

As the two friends talked about what had happened later on in the day, they both recalled how Sam had shared with them his burden for his son, Tom, who was the only one of his five children who had not yet accepted Christ as his Savior.

Tom's wife Julie had become a Christian through the testimony of Tom's parents. She and their three children had often been abused by Tom, who was addicted to alcohol. There were times when she would take the children and go to Tom's parents' house for the night because of his abuse. Now Tom had started on drugs, causing an even greater burden to his family.

The large church building was packed for the funeral. Sam and Edna West had many friends. Pastor Johnson presented the gospel as clearly as he possibly could. Sam had previously mentioned to the pastor that whenever God called him home, he wanted the gospel to be preached at his funeral service.

Tom sat between his mother and his wife, Julie. He was nervous and uncomfortable as Pastor Johnson spoke about God's provision for a lost human race through His beloved Son, Jesus.

"I don't know how much of this I can take," whispered Tom to Julie. "I know I'm not the man I should be, and those things that the pastor is saying are only making me feel worse." Tom was glad when the service was over and the burial was completed. He felt that the day, even though it was very difficult, was good for him, as he had made some secret decisions in his own heart.

That night, after they returned home, Tom spoke to his wife as he had not done in years. "I'm sorry, Julie, for the way I've acted these past years. I know I don't believe in God the way you do, but at least I can try to change my habits and live a better life and try to give you and our three children a better home."

That night Julie knelt beside the bed as she had always done since she was saved and prayed once more that God would save Tom.

Tom received a phone call from Phil Thompson just a week later. "Tom," said Phil, "as you know, your dad played a lot of golf with Ed Jones and me. I know that you are a good deal younger than we are, but how about going around the golf course with us on Saturday morning, if you're free?"

Tom was taken aback for a moment by Phil's request, but after a slight hesitancy, he told Phil that he was free and would join the men. Julie, hearing that Tom was golfing with his dad's two best friends, felt in her heart that this was all ordered by the Lord, Who would use it for His glory.

"I think that's great, honey," said Julie, "but just one thing . . . don't you let those old fellows beat you or you'll never hear the end of it, at least from me."

Tom West began to see some things happen in his life. His decision to stop drinking and taking drugs improved his home relationship immediately. Now, for some reason, his father's two best friends and golfing companions called and asked him to go golfing with them. A feeling of excitement began to build within Tom, an excitement that he truly did not understand.

Saturday morning came, and Tom met Ed Jones and Phil Thompson at the golf course at the appointed time. Tom was a much better player than the other two men, and this showed immediately.

"Hey there, Tom, your dad at least gave us a chance! You're going to walk away with this game if you don't slow down!" The three men talked and laughed as they made their way around the course. They finally arrived at the seventh hole.

Tom, who had parred the sixth hole, led off. He knew exactly what had happened at that very same spot just ten days before. Ed and Phil could feel the tension that the younger man was under. They stood silent as he approached the area to tee off. Tom, with his number-one wood in his left hand, bent down to press the tee into the ground. He hesitated a moment and then sank to his knees.

"Fellows," he said in a broken voice, "I can't go on this way. I know better, and I need to do something about it right here and now."

Ed and Phil hurried to Tom's side. They both knelt beside him. Phil asked Tom if he was ready to acknowledge his lost condition and receive Christ as his Savior.

"I am, Phil," spoke Tom. "I need Him more than anything else in the world. Will you pray with me?" The three men bowed their heads as Phil prayed while Tom asked Christ to save him.

As Tom stood to his feet, he pointed to the ground where he had been kneeling. "That is where Dad went home to be with the Lord, and I came to know the Lord. I'll remember this place as long as I live."

The men then headed immediately for the clubhouse, where Tom called Julie to tell her of his salvation at the seventh hole.

EYES BUT CAN'T SEE

What is this country known for besides being poverty-stricken and landlocked in the heart of Africa?" The visiting American waited for an answer to his very pointed question.

Dale Compton thought for a moment before he began to speak. Jim, though not a Christian, had come to appreciate the close friendship of the missionaries as he traveled far from home. Dale and Ann and their co-workers, Tom and Marie Page, had prayed for opportunities to witness to him, but Jim had not seemed receptive.

"There are two other things, Jim. First, I just read a magazine article last week about this country. Would you believe that we are the butterfly capital of the world?"

"Yes, I can believe that," answered the tourist. "What's the second thing?"

"Well," replied Dale with a frown, "we also have the largest variety of poisonous snakes of any country in the world."

"Wow! You can keep that title," Jim laughed. "I don't like snakes of any kind or size."

Dale looked at his watch. "Sorry to leave you, Jim, but I've got to service my car and give it an oil change."

Within minutes, the veteran missionary was down in the car pit getting ready to start work on his vehicle.

because Dale was only five feet, six inches tall, he had to stand on a box in the deep pit. Beside him was his faithful African worker, Pierre. Dale hummed as he worked.

While unscrewing the oil drain plug, Dale felt something strike his right ankle. Because there wasn't any pain, he didn't even think about it. However, his thoughts turned to the conversation with Jim and the grim reality passed through his mind.

"A snake!" he whispered to himself as he stepped down from the box. He put his right foot up on one of the steps leading out of the pit. Pulling down his sock, he immediately spotted two tiny red marks on the outside anklebone. He looked up at Pierre who stood watching from the other end of the pit.

"Pierre, what are these two small red marks on my ankle?"

The African looked, then glanced around the pit. "That's a snakebite, Mr. Compton."

"But it doesn't hurt," said Dale, his voice showing some concern.

"Believe me, Mr. Compton," responded Pierre, "it's a snakebite."

Pierre kicked over the small box on which Dale had been standing and discovered a small black spitting cobra.

"That's the snake that bit you," affirmed the African.

Dale had seen cobra bites before and knew what they could do to the victims. "Pierre, call Mr. Page and tell him to come quickly with his car. I have to go to the hospital."

Fifteen minutes later, Dale and his coworker, Tom Page, arrived at the emergency room of the city hospital. Pierre walked behind them, carrying the dead snake by the tail.

"Is that the snake that bit you?" asked the African nurse. "Quickly, get up on the table."

The nurse then proceeded to inject Dale with 20 cc of antivenom serum. She gave three injections around the bite, one right above his knee and the rest of the serum in his hip. Dale noticed that the girl wiped the needle off with her fingers after each injection. He glanced at Tom, who watched in disbelief.

Dale wanted to say something to the hospital worker but held back, realizing that he was at her mercy. He had often heard of the poor treatment given at the hospital and now he was experiencing it.

Back at the mission station, Dale and Tom told what happened. "I wouldn't be surprised if I came down with something from that contaminated needle," Dale concluded.

Jim was astonished at what he heard. "I've got to hand it to you people. I sure couldn't do what you're doing."

Three days later Dale awoke with a fever. A red streak ran partly up his leg. A rash appeared in the areas where he had received the injections. After breakfast, he drove to the hospital where he asked to see a French doctor. He explained what had taken place at the emergency room three days earlier.

"Some of the hospital workers have come out of very primitive areas," spoke the doctor, "and we just can't get it across to them that germs do exist even though they can't see them with their eyes."

The doctor prescribed antibiotics for Dale. "You'll be all right in a few days, Pastor. If you have any problems, come back and see me."

Jim had accompanied Dale to the hospital and was waiting for him when he came out of the doctor's office. They talked about the incident on the way home.

"This thing that happened, Jim, reminds me of those who don't have Christ as their Savior," spoke Dale.

"How is that?" questioned Jim.

"Well, Christ through His death provided salvation for them. Because they can't see it, many will not believe. We both know it's a proven fact that germs exist. The microscope reveals that. God's existence is proven in many ways too. Man only has to believe the proven facts."

"I see," replied Jim. "One of those proven facts is the life of each of you missionaries, am I correct?" Before Dale could answer, Jim continued, "You missionaries have shown me that you are different. I know you have something that I don't have."

Dale spoke softly. "It is Christ Whom we have in our hearts, Jim. It would be wonderful if He was your Savior too."

Dale prayed silently that Jim would accept Christ before he left them to continue his tour. He felt real gratitude to the Lord that their lives reflected Christ in such a wonderful way.

DISTANT SINGING

Children's voices singing in the distance caused Bill to stop and listen. He placed the paper bag he was carrying on the bench beside him. He had just made his daily trip through that section of the city, rummaging in the trash cans and dumpsters outside business establishments. It was an unusually successful day for Bill as he had found one half of a roasted chicken someone had thrown out. Usually he fed on scraps of food which he found here and there.

He heard off in the distance the singing of a familiar song:

> Jesus loves me, this I know.
> For the Bible tells me so.
> Little ones to Him belong.
> They are weak, but He is strong.

Tears came to his eyes as he continued to listen. His thoughts flashed back to his boyhood days when his Christian mother taught him that very same chorus when he began talking. Bill Rhodes was born of Christian parents and grew up in a home that honored God. In those early days it seemed as though he lived in church. His family was there every time the doors were open. For any of the Rhodes family to miss a church service was a serious matter.

Bill wiped the tears from his face with his rough, calloused fingers. He recalled the day that he asked his father what it meant to be saved. He could still see the serious look upon his father's face as he spoke to him.

"God says in the Bible that we are sinners, and because we are sinners there is a penalty that we must pay. That penalty, Billy, is to be away from God forever. The Bible speaks of a place called hell, which is a fire which burns forever. That is where sinners go who don't believe in Jesus as their Savior."

"I don't want to go there, Daddy," spoke Billy. "I want to be in Heaven with you and Mommy and Jesus."

"You can go there, Billy, by asking Jesus to forgive you of your sins and to save you," spoke his father. He reached out and put his arms around his son. "Billy, would you like to ask Jesus to come into your life now and save you?"

"I do, Daddy. I want to do it now," responded Billy, wiping a tear from his eye. Together the father and son bowed their heads while Billy prayed, asking God to save him.

As Bill grew into his teenage years, something happened. He began dating one of his high school friends who was not a Christian. Rose Martin was a beautiful girl who was voted senior class queen. She excelled in her studies as well as in sports. Little by little Bill stopped going to church until finally he was not going at all. He began staying out until the early morning hours. Some nights he would not come home at all. At first his parents only smelled alcohol on his breath. It wasn't long until he was coming home drunk.

"Bill," said his father one night after his son came home smelling of alcohol, "I want to help you, Son. Is there something that I can do for you?"

"I don't need your help, Dad. There's nothing wrong with me. You and Mom are the ones who need the help. You're so old-fashioned in the way you think."

John Rhodes had never heard his son speak to him like that before. The words pierced his heart like a spear. "I love you, Bill," continued his father. "I don't want to see you ruin your life, Son, and I'll do anything that I possibly can to help you."

The next week Bill Rhodes married his high school girlfriend and disappeared out of his parents' lives. John and Elsie Rhodes were heartbroken for their only child. They had no idea where he had gone or how they could contact him.

Three years after their marriage, Bill and Rose were divorced. They had a baby boy whom they named William, after his father. After the divorce was granted, both mother and son vanished, leaving Bill Rhodes alone without any contact with his family. He tried various places to find work but was unsuccessful. He finally joined others like himself who didn't have work or a home. He lived on the streets, finding shelter where he could. Eight years had now passed since his wife had taken their son and left. Bill Rhodes was a lonely man.

> Yes, Jesus loves me.
> Yes, Jesus loves me.
> Yes, Jesus loves me.
> The Bible tells me so.

Once again he heard the words of the children as they sang.

Bill picked up his paper bag and started in the opposite direction from the singing. He took several steps and stopped.

"I can't go on this way," he said to himself. "Those words speak the truth. God does love me. I'm the one who turned against Him. I put Him out of my life. Oh, God," he cried, "help me to get my life straightened out. I want to come back to You."

Bill followed the voices of the children and came to an apartment building where they had gathered in one of the apartments. As he stood outside, a man came out of the house with a Bible in his hands.

"Sir," called Bill, "can I speak with you please?" The man stopped and then came over to where Bill was standing.

"What can I do for you?" he asked.

Bill told him the story of his life. He mentioned how he had accepted Jesus as his Savior as a child and of the catastrophe of his marriage. The stranger stood and listened and then asked Bill to accompany him to a restaurant down the street. The men entered the restaurant, taking a booth in the rear of the room. There they talked and ate. Bill had not had a meal like that in years. The man was a pastor of a small church in the neighborhood and had come to speak to the children at a vacation Bible school class which was being held for children living in the apartments.

With his head bowed, Bill Rhodes prayed, asking God to forgive him and to help him. When the two men left the restaurant, the pastor took Bill Rhodes home with him. The first thing he did upon entering the house was to call his parents and tell them what had happened.

"Thank the Lord for this answer to prayer," said Bill's mother. "We've been trying to reach you because we have some wonderful news for you too. Rose came back to her parents and a few weeks later accepted Christ as her Savior. She tried to locate you, but you had moved, and no one knew where you went. Your dad and I see Rose and Billy practically every day. We spend a lot of time together."

Bill Rhodes could hardly believe what he was hearing. "God is so good," he said in a whisper to his parents who were talking to him on extension phones. "I thought I had lost Rose and Billy, and here all the time they have been back there near you."

Arrangements were made for Bill to fly back home. The pastor made a few phone calls to some of the families in the church, and within fifteen minutes he had more than sufficient funds to pay for Bill's ticket. Early the next morning Bill Rhodes boarded a plane for home. The past twelve hours had brought a tremendous change in his life.

"I'll send you the money just as soon as I get a job," said Bill to the pastor.

"No, you don't have to do that, Bill. Your ticket is a gift of love to you from God's people. We're just happy to have the privilege of a tiny part in it all."

Bill Rhodes was filled with excitement as he walked into the airport lobby. The same size as the pastor, he had been given a complete outfit, including shoes, by his new friend. He spotted Rose immediately with his son, Billy, standing beside her. Her parents and his parents stood behind them. They rushed toward each other. Billy only slightly remembered his daddy, but the resemblance between the two was unmistakeable. Tears flowed as they embraced each other.

"Honey, will you marry me?" Bill whispered into Rose's ear.

"Just as soon as possible," she responded. "That's the Lord's will for us, Bill."

That night was the closing service for the vacation Bible school. Bill sat between the two sets of parents with Rose and Billy. He held Rose's hand tightly as he listened to the opening chorus sung by a group of the smaller children.

>Jesus loves me, this I know.
>For the Bible tells me so.
>Little ones to Him belong.
>They are weak, but He is strong.
>Yes, Jesus loves me.
>Yes, Jesus loves me.
>Yes, Jesus loves me.
>The Bible tells me so.

Rose turned and looked at Bill. "That's our song, Bill, and it will be for the rest of our lives together."

A NEW BEGINNING

I can't do it, Tom," Ed pleaded. "I can't hurt that old man. I've known him all my life."

Tom swung hard and landed a blow to the side of Ed's head. The 18-year-old fell forward, striking his chin on the concrete floor.

"No one talks to me like that," grunted the gang leader, rubbing the knuckles on his right hand. "When Tom King tells you to do something, you do it! Understand what I'm saying, Ed?"

Half dazed from the blows on the side of his head and jaw, Ed nodded agreement with what the gang leader had said.

More than once, Ed Moore had asked himself what he was doing in a gang like the Scorpions. Raised in a Christian home where the Bible was read and honored and where God's name was sacred, he had gone to church and Sunday School on a regular basis right up to the time he had left home fourteen months ago. He was so much involved in crimes the gang had committed that he knew he would be convicted if he ever was found or turned himself in to the authorities. Seven months had passed since his last contact with his parents—a short phone call to see how they were doing.

After spitting on Ed, Tom walked out of the room without saying another word. The entire gang dreaded his tirades and did everything they could to keep him happy and avoid his vicious beatings.

A veteran of the gang, Tiny Wolfe, went to Ed's assistance. "You just don't talk back to Tom. You're lucky to be alive, Ed," said the gang member as he helped Ed to his feet. Tiny was by far the biggest and strongest member of the gang.

"I'll walk with you to your room, Ed," Tiny decided. "You took two heavy blows just now. You'll want to get a cold, wet cloth on those swollen places."

Ed had the smallest room of the gang, about six by eight feet. A dim unshaded light bulb hung from the ceiling. Ed had just lain down when Tom walked in.

"Get up on your feet, kid," snapped the gang leader. "I have a job for you to do, and you'd better not slip up on it."

Ed got off the little cot as fast as he could move. His head was throbbing with pain from the blows of Tom's fists.

"What do you want me to do, Tom?" asked Ed, his voice quivering from fear.

"I want you to go to that old man's house. Wait till after dark and wear a mask so he won't recognize you. Get the money he has stashed away in that castle. Before you leave, tie him up and gag him. And, Ed, I want to read in the papers that you worked the old guy over real well. I want you to do a job on him. This will teach the other old people on our list not to give us any opposition when we visit them."

Ed's knees felt weak. He wanted to tell Tom that Mr. Parker had been his Sunday School teacher and was like a father to him. He knew, however, that such talk would only infuriate the gang leader even more.

That evening Ed drove the gang's car to the neighborhood where Mr. Parker lived. As he drove down the street, he recognized several people. He hoped they did not recognize him. He parked the car far down the street and nervously made his way to the elderly man's house. By the time he reached his destination, it was almost dark. By a light in the front room, Ed could see Mr. Parker reading the newspaper. He stepped softly as he went up to the front steps and crossed the porch to the door.

Pushing the doorbell button, Ed looked through the window to see Mr. Parker put down his paper and head for the door. Ed was scared. He could feel the perspiration on his forehead. The stocking mask was still in his back pocket.

"Yes, can I help you?" inquired Mr. Parker in a kind voice.

He took another look at Ed and smiled in surprise, reaching out to shake Ed's hand. "Why, Ed Moore! What a surprise to see you. Come in."

Ed stepped into the house as Mr. Parker closed the door behind him. "I haven't seen you for at least two years. How have you been? How are your parents?"

"I'm fine, thank you," answered Ed. The feeling of the father-son relationship began to haunt him. He thought of Tom's words, "I want to read in the papers that you worked the old guy over real well."

"Well, Ed, you haven't changed much. You are bigger, but otherwise you look the same," said Mr. Parker. "Tell me, what have you been doing with yourself?"

The words struck Ed like a sledgehammer. How could he ever tell the truth about himself? What would his former Sunday School teacher say if he told him that he had quit school and left home, and for the past fourteen months he had been part of a gang which robbed and assaulted people?

A strange feeling came over Ed. He knew he had to answer Mr. Parker's questions somehow. He didn't want to lie to his friend, yet he was embarrassed to tell the truth. Ed's eyes filled with tears. He tried to hide them, but it was too late. His former Sunday School teacher saw them and knew there was something wrong.

"What is it, Ed?" he asked quietly. "There's something bothering you, isn't there?"

Ed tried to speak, but the lump in his throat made it difficult for him.

"I . . . I . . . I need help, Mr. Parker," he admitted slowly. "I'm not living right. I left Mom and Dad over a year ago and joined a gang. We live over on the west side of the city. I've done a lot of bad things—things that I thought I would never do. I've robbed . . . ."

"Ed," interrupted the older man, "are you in trouble with the law?"

"Yes, I am, Mr. Parker," answered Ed without any hesitancy. "I've been dodging the police for a year."

"You belong to the Lord, Ed," said Mr. Parker. "I watched you respond to the things of the Lord for several years. God has given to you talents which you can use for Him. You need to get right with the Lord, Son.

The two men talked some more and finally slipped to their knees. Ed confessed his sinful ways and asked God to forgive him. The elderly man hugged Ed when they stood to their feet.

"I've got to call Mom and Dad," said Ed, drying his eyes and looking around for the phone. "They'll be so happy to hear that God has answered their prayers tonight."

Later that night, Ed, along with his father and Mr. Parker, appeared at the police station. He told the police of his involvement in past crimes. An officer placed him under arrest. As Ed's father left his son, he placed his arm around him.

"I know this is not what any of us wanted, Ed," he spoke with mixed emotions, "but I'm happy that you have returned to the Lord. You know that we will help you in any way that we possibly can. You have a new start, even if that start is serving a jail sentence for your crimes."

"It's been a hard lesson, Dad," admitted Ed, trying not to cry, "but I want it to be a very valuable lesson. I want my life to count for God from now on."

Ed Moore was on his way with a new beginning.

GOOD OUT OF BAD
(Based on a True Experience)

"Tom, have you seen my sunglasses? I've looked for them everywhere."

Lois White stood in the doorway of the little three-room building which was home to the Whites. Tom looked out from underneath the hood of the pickup truck where he had been working most of the morning.

"I haven't seen them, Lois. When did you have them last?"

"Well, I know I had them when I went to class this morning," said Lois, looking somewhat puzzled. "I did stop over at Betty's to talk with her. I wonder if I left them there?"

Tom and Lois were in the middle of their first term of missionary service. Since the age of eight, Lois had wanted to be a missionary to Africa. The couple had met in Bible college and were married shortly after Lois graduated.

Since there was not a vacant house on the mission station when the Whites arrived, they moved into a combination garage and storehouse. The young couple worked hard at making their unusual living quarters look as much like a home as possible.

The search for the missing sunglasses became the topic of conversation among the missionaries. Several of the

African Christians also looked for them along the path where Lois could have lost them. After three days of searching, Tom and Lois decided that the glasses would probably not be found.

"Someone has no doubt picked them up and either sold them or sent them to a relative in some distant village," Tom suggested.

"A lot of good that will do them," responded Lois. "Since they are prescription sunglasses, the person wouldn't be able to see with them."

Even though the situation seemed hopeless, Lois prayed that the Lord would help her get her glasses back. Some of the women in her Bible class were also praying for the return of the glasses.

Two weeks after the sunglasses had disappeared, one of the missionaries, Bud Stone, was on his way to the Bible school building to conduct a class. Hearing someone call to him, he turned to see an African whom he did not recognize advancing toward him.

"Hello there," called Bud. "What can I do for you?"

The African reached into his pocket and pulled out a pair of sunglasses in a case. The name Lois White was printed on the case.

"My eyes can't see straight with these glasses, Mister," spoke the stranger. "Can you fix them for me so I can see with them? If you can't do that , then I will have to sell them to someone."

"Where did you get those glasses?" asked the surprised missionary.

"I found them along that path over there," he answered. "I saw them come out of a bag that a lady missionary was carrying."

"But didn't you realize that the glasses belonged to her? Why didn't you call her and give them to her?"

"Well, Mister, we believe that when someone loses something, the thing wants to get away from that person. Those glasses didn't want to stay in that woman's bag. That's why they jumped out onto the path."

Bud rubbed his forehead. Now he'd heard everything! He took the glasses and told the man to wait for him outside the school building until his class was over.

Later on, Bud and the African went to find Tom and Lois. As he told the story, the young couple stood in silence. Each day brought strange new things into their lives, but this seemed to top them all.

One by one Africans joined the group to hear what was being said. Finally, one of the deacons of the church spoke.

"What he is saying is not true. Our people do not believe that way. He made up that story for you missionaries."

The deacon looked closely at the man. "You stole those glasses, didn't you? They didn't jump out of Mrs. White's bag. You got close enough to her so you could pick them out of the bag with your own hands. Am I not speaking the truth?"

The African knew that he could not deceive his fellow tribesmen. He knew he was caught. He looked down at the ground. "You are right. I did take the glasses. I didn't realize that the other missionaries would know they were missing. I knew they are the kind that the missionaries wear, and I thought I could wear them or even sell them."

"Mrs. White's name is right there on the case," continued the deacon. "You didn't know it because you can't read. What is your name?"

"Mbate," spoke the African. "My name is Mbate. I come by here to go to the river. I have some fish traps there."

"Well, Mbate, I think you should come here to class and learn to read and write. We would tell you about Jesus too," the deacon offered.

The African's face glowed with excitement to think of his newly found friends and the fact that he was not penalized for the wrong he had done. He was glad, too, for the invitation to attend class.

The next day, Mbate arrived for class. Bud enjoyed seeing the interest of his new student. Three days after he started attending classes, Mbate accepted Christ as his Savior.

"God," he prayed, seated with Bud under a tree outside the classroom building, "I don't know much about You yet. I know that You love me and that Jesus, Your Son, died for me. God, forgive me of my sins and make me Your child."

Mbate became a close friend of the missionaries in the months that followed. In a testimony at church one day he referred to the glasses that he had stolen.

"God can make good come out of bad. I stole Mrs. White's glasses and later tried to have them fixed by one of her missionary coworkers. I would have even sold them to him."

The Africans laughed at Mbate's remark.

"I'm glad I didn't know very much then. If I had been able to read, I would not have brought them back. But God took that bad thing which I had done and used it to bring me to know Jesus as my Savior."

LOST

Sandy felt faint at the telephone message from the Sunday School superintendent. He was calling from the park, where several of the classes were picnicking, to report that Sandy's nine-year-old daughter, Brenda, was missing.

Sandy regained her composure and called Pastor Comstock. "I just received the news, Sandy." There was concern in the kind pastor's voice. "You stay there. Ann and I are coming right over. The police have been notified and are already searching for her."

Sandy and Mike Price had both become Christians at an early age in vacation Bible school. High school sweethearts, they were married the day after graduation from college.

People in the church considered Sandy and Mike to have the perfect romance. Both were very mature, and their pleasant personalities brought many friends into their lives. Two years after marriage, they were blessed with a baby girl whom they named Brenda. Like her parents, she also had a sweet disposition and was loved by all.

The church family was shocked when Mike drowned during a fishing outing. Brenda had celebrated her seventh birthday two days before.

Sandy was standing in the doorway when the pastor and his wife arrived. "Thank you for coming over," she said nervously. "Do you think we could go out to the park? Maybe we could help in the search."

The distraught mother could not hold back the tears any longer. She tried to speak, but the words would not come. Ann put her arm around Sandy to comfort her.

Thirty minutes later, the pastor, his wife and Sandy arrived at the park. Several police cars were there; some of the police had gone into the forest with trained dogs.

The church bus, used to transport the children, had already left to take the children back to their parents at the church. The superintendent, along with a number of men from the church, remained to join the search.

A police captain came to speak with Sandy. "This particular wooded area is not too large, Mrs. Price—only about a mile through at the most. Our dogs will find your daughter if she's in there."

"If she's in there," Sandy repeated softly to herself. "Dear Lord, let her be in there and help the men to find her."

The captain had not reflected all of his thoughts in what he had said. He had already confided to the pastor, when the two were alone for a few minutes, that he had some fears about the missing girl. An escaped kidnapper and murderer from the state prison had been seen in the area the day before.

"Captain," spoke Sandy, "would you mind if Pastor Comstock prayed for the searchers and for Brenda?"

"Not at all, Mrs. Price," replied the tall police officer. "Those searchers need all the help they can get."

The captain removed his hat and bowed his head along with the others.

"Father," began the pastor, "there are things which You allow to come into our lives that we don't understand. We know that You love us, and all things do work together for good to those who love You. We ask You, Father, to bring Brenda safely back to us. Lead the men to her, and may she be safe."

Ten minutes later, one of the policemen came running out of the woods. "Captain," he called, "we found a shoe and it has blood . . . ." The policeman, when he saw Sandy beside the captain, did not finish what he was saying.

Sandy looked at the little shoe with blood on the side of it. "That's Brenda's shoe, Captain," she said in a whisper. "God is able to bring my little girl back to me, and I still believe He will do that."

The police captain had witnessed many tragedies in his years on the force, but this was one case that was entirely different. He could not understand the faith of a mother who believed God would return her daughter alive and well—even with a blood-marked shoe as evidence to the contrary.

"I admire you, Mrs. Price," replied the captain. "You're a brave woman with a lot of faith."

It was dark before Sandy realized it. The huge floodlights from two emergency vehicles lit the area. Sandy noticed the concerned faces of the pastor and Ann. Even the captain grew increasingly tense.

"There comes someone now," said Sandy, pointing to a light bobbing through the trees.

"There are several of them," added the captain, "and they are carrying something."

"It's Brenda!" shouted Sandy, running to meet the men.

Fearing the worst, the police officer ran after her. "Mrs. Price! Wait here. She may need medical help and we must stay out of the way of the medics!"

The excited mother stopped at the captain's request.

"It's all right, Captain," called one of the men. "The girl is fine. She's frightened, but she's okay."

"Mommy!" called Brenda. "I lost my shoe."

The little girl's remark broke the tension. Even the captain joined in with a hearty laugh.

"Oh, honey, I'm so glad to see you. Are you all right?" questioned Sandy.

"I'm all right, Mommy," Brenda answered. "I got lost. Some of us were looking for flowers under the trees. We saw a snake, and I thought it was chasing me. I ran a long way, and when I stopped, the other girls were gone."

"How did you lose your shoe, Brenda?" asked the captain, examining a long scratch on her leg.

"I started calling for help when I heard something in the leaves. I thought it was the snake. I began to run again and tripped over something. My shoe came off, but I was afraid to stop and pick it up."

Brenda shielded her eyes from the bright lights. "Mommy, can we go home?"

"We sure can, honey," answered the happy mother, taking her daughter by the hand and heading for the pastor's car.

The medics cleaned the scratch and placed a small bandage over it. The captain promised Pastor Comstock that he would come to church the next day. "I want to learn more about the kind of faith I saw here today," he asserted. "God did answer your Mommy's prayers, Brenda. You have both convinced me that you must have a special relationship with God."

"We do, Captain." Sandy spoke serenely. "We really do."

SOMETHING VERY SPECIAL

John noticed the worn lining in his coat as he removed it from the hanger. He glanced over at his wife, Carol, who stood watching sadly.

"Cheer up, honey," said John, forcing a smile. "I'm sure it has another year's wear in it."

John and Carol Grant had arrived home from the interior of Brazil just a month before. They had managed to get through their first term of service with a minimum of support. Ever since their marriage, the couple had been extremely careful in their expenditures. Carol had a knack for making food stretch, and even though the Grants did not have very much, their house was always neat and clean.

"You need a new suit, honey," Carol responded, running her hand across John's shoulders. "Let's take the money we were saving for tires for the car. A suit is more important now."

John smiled at his wife. "Let's wait a bit, Carol. Maybe the Lord will provide a suit for me."

The young husband packed the bags for his weekend ministry into the trunk of the car. Before leaving the house, he and Carol bowed their heads while John prayed, committing themselves and his ministry during the short missionary conference to the Lord.

As John drove along the highway, his thoughts went back home to Carol. He remembered how she prayed before he left that the Lord would supply a suit for him. His eyes moistened with tears as he thought of the faithful companion God had given him.

As John pulled up to the church, he saw a middle-aged man walking across the parking lot.

"I take it you are John Grant," the man greeted him with a smile. "I am Pastor Shultz. Welcome to Grace Baptist Church."

John reached out and shook the pastor's hand. He noticed the kindness that showed through the deep blue eyes of the pastor.

John took his bags out of the car and walked with the pastor next door to the parsonage. The pastor's wife met them at the door.

"It's nice to meet you, Mr. Grant. My husband will take you to your room. We will have supper in thirty minutes, if that is all right with you."

John blinked as he walked into the bright blue bedroom. Everything was so beautiful. He looked at the king-size bed before him, amazed at its size.

"When you're ready, come downstairs," said the pastor.

John began to feel right at home with his new friends.

That night at the church, John told about his conversion and how God had led him to Bible school where he had met the woman he married. He told of their deputation ministry and described their arrival in Brazil and how they worked to win the hearts of the people.

At the close of the service, three young men came forward to dedicate their lives to the Lord for missionary service.

"Praise the Lord, John!" exclaimed Pastor Shultz. "We have been praying for those three men for many months."

Just before John went up to his room, the pastor met with him alone in the kitchen.

"John," he announced excitedly, "the chairman of our men's fellowship came to me after the service tonight to say the men would like to do something special for you. Do you have something in mind for them? I might add that one of them own's a men's store, if you are interested in clothing."

John thought of Carol's prayer just before he left home that afternoon.

"The men's store sounds good to me, Pastor," admitted the visitor. "I really don't have many good clothes."

"Great!" responded Pastor Shultz. "Tomorrow morning after breakfast, you and I will visit Pete's Clothing Store."

John Grant entered his room and fell to his knees beside his bed.

"Father, thank You for Your goodness. Thank You for touching the hearts of these men to do this for me."

The next morning, John went with Pastor Shultz to the men's clothing store.

"Good morning," called Pete Cooper, stepping out from behind the counter. "How are Pastor and our missionary friend today?"

"Just fine," answered Pastor Shultz, smiling. "What do you have in this store, Pete, that will fit John?"

The next hour was spent trying on suits, slacks and sport coats. By the time Pete had finished, John had two suits, two pairs of slacks, two sport coats, six dress shirts and six ties. Pete added six pairs of socks to the collection of clothes.

John stood in amazement. Pastor Shultz and Pete silently watched the missionary as he wiped the tears from his eyes.

"I'm at a loss for words," spoke John. "I've never had anything like this happen to me before."

On the way home, Pastor Shultz stopped at a shoe store where the missionary was instructed to purchase a pair of dress shoes.

Arriving back at the parsonage, John immediately called Carol. "Honey, this news is almost too good to be true." The excited missionary then related to his wife all that had taken place. "And to think that the suits will be tailored today and will be delivered here at Pastor

Shultz's house before the service begins tonight."

"We have a wonderful God, John," replied Carol. "Praise the Lord for those men."

"I'll see you tomorrow night, Carol," spoke the happy husband. "I plan to leave right after church."

"Drive carefully, honey," cautioned Carol. "Remember those tires aren't the best."

The phone rang as soon as John hung up. Pastor Shultz answered.

"Hi, Charlie. You want to do what?" The pastor listened intently and then spoke. "I'm sure he won't mind. Here, I'll let you talk to him."

John took the phone. "Hello, this is John Grant."

"Brother Grant, I own a tire store. Today I happened to notice your tires when I came by the church for something; you know, they aren't safe to drive on."

"I know they are bad," answered John.

"Well," continued the caller, "after the evening service tonight, would you drive over to my store? It won't take long. I want to replace all your tires."

John stood speechless. Finally he stammered, "Thank you, dear brother. I will be happy to drive over."

John stood in silence after he put down the phone. He recalled Carol's words about his worn suit and how they could use the money they were saving to buy tires.

"Thank You, Lord," he whispered. "Thank You for the clothing and the tires which You provided through these wonderful people."

That night, after the tires had been replaced, John left for home. As he drove along, his heart was filled with thanksgiving for the blessings of the past two days. He thought of the sewing machine for which Carol had been praying. Now that the Lord had provided the tires for the car, he decided to surprise her by suggesting that the tire funds be used for that. He drove into the driveway about midnight. Carol came out on the porch to meet him.

"Praise the Lord, honey," said John as he opened the car door. "What a blessed weekend this has been."

As they walked into the house together, Carol smiled

up at her husband. "Does this mean that we can use the tire money to buy the sewing machine?"

"It sure does," answered John, hugging his wife. "God has made that possible by doing something very special for us."

LOVE AND CARE
(Based on a True Story)

You can believe that lie if you want. Just don't expect me to go along with it!" shouted Jan, slamming the bedroom door behind her.

Harry Frost had told his wife about his decision to accept Christ as his Savior. For the past three Sundays he had been attending the little Baptist church in their small rural community. That morning, he had responded to the invitation and had gone forward to profess his faith in Christ publicly.

Harry stood silently in the hallway, somewhat shocked at Jan's tirade. He certainly had not meant to upset his wife so.

Finally, he decided to attempt talking to her through the closed door. "Jan," called Harry softly, "please don't be angry. Can't we just sit down and talk about this?"

"For three weeks now you have gone to that . . . that nuthouse," replied Jan bitterly. "I told you that I didn't want you to go there. Now you come home and tell me they've sold you on their religious garbage and that you are saved—whatever that means."

The week that followed was an extremely difficult time for Harry and Jan. More than once, she threatened to take their two children and leave him. Wherever she went in town, she spoke out against the Baptist church and its "heretical" beliefs. She told anyone who would listen how Harry's new religion was breaking up their marriage.

The people at Calvary Baptist Church heard Jan's remarks against them and vowed to pray for her even more. Harry continued to attend the church services but was not able to take their two children with him. He found the door locked several times when he arrived home from church, but he would wait patiently outside until Jan would allow one of the children to let him in.

The situation worsened daily for the Frosts. Finally, Jan told Harry that either he would have to go or she would leave. Their two children—Amy, age seven, and Paul, age five—were beginning to show the effects of living under such a poor relationship between their parents.

Pastor Bridges was in his study when he received the phone call. "Did you hear the news about the Frosts, Pastor?" asked Dick Grange, one of the deacons.

"No, I haven't, Dick," replied the pastor. "What have you heard?"

The deacon went on to tell Pastor Bridges that the doctor had diagnosed Amy as having infectious hepatitis and had quarantined the family for two weeks.

No sooner had Dick hung up than the phone rang again. This time it was Marge Miller, president of the Ladies Fellowship group.

"What do you think about the ladies in the church furnishing meals to the Frost family until the quarantine is lifted?" inquired Marge. There was excitement in her voice as she spoke. "Here is one way we can be a help to the family and show Jan that we love her."

The pastor thought the idea was a good one and said the sooner the women got started, the better.

In minutes Marge was on the phone with Jan Frost. "I'm sorry to hear about Amy being sick, Jan," spoke Marge, who knew Jan better than any of the other women in the church. "The ladies of the church want to help you out, and one way we can is to provide meals for your family."

The telephone call took Jan by surprise. She was at a loss for words. "Well, uh, thank you, Marge. You know, that can mean a lot of meals," said Jan hesitantly.

"Oh, that's all right, Jan," continued Marge. "There are several of us, and it isn't that much of a job. Really, Jan, we want to do this for you, Harry and the children."

By the time the telephone called ended, Jan Frost was amazed by the generous commitment of the women in the church to supply all their meals for the extent of the quarantine.

That evening the first meal arrived. One of the ladies drove into the drive, placed the food on the porch just outside the door and returned to her car. Jan looked out of the window just in time to get a big smile and a friendly wave of the hand. She smiled and waved back. During the next two weeks, Jan received daily smiles and waves from the women as they faithfully delivered the meals.

An increasing number of telephone calls also came from the ladies to Jan, inquiring how things were going and if her family had any food preferences. The love and care of the Ladies Fellowship group was something Jan could not understand. Harry knew that something was happening in his wife's heart as he observed her response to the women from the church.

Pastor Bridges arrived home from hospital visitation two weeks later to find a car in the drive. He parked behind it and entered the house through the back door. He heard voices coming from the front room, where his wife, Mary, and Jan Frost were on their knees.

"Oh, God," sobbed Jan, "please forgive me of all my sins. I've done so many wicked things. Save me and make me like Harry. I need You, Lord."

When the two women finished praying, they got to their feet.

"Thank you, Mrs. Bridges," said Jan, throwing her arms around Mary. "You women have been so kind to me."

Jan then saw the pastor standing in the doorway. "Pastor Bridges, I just accepted Jesus as my Savior. I'm so happy, I hardly know what to say!"

Pastor Bridges clasped Jan's hand. "The women were thankful for the opportunity to help you and your family, Jan. This was their way to serve the Lord."

"I'm glad that Amy's sickness wasn't as bad as we thought at first," Jan said, wiping the tears away as she spoke, "but I am so thankful that it all happened. God used it to bring me to Him. And Pastor, my Harry was so kind through it all. I don't know how he put up with my meanness, but he did."

The next Sunday, Pastor Bridges smiled at the Frost family sitting in the second row. Harry smiled back and winked. Jan dabbed at her eyes with her handkerchief. She never knew that she could be so happy. Amy had fully recovered. Jan now was a Christian, her family was together, and she had many friends in her new church home.

UNPLEASANT BLESSING

"Did stagecoaches really travel over this road, Mr. Bently?" Karen's blue eyes literally sparkled as the eight-year-old questioned her Sunday School teacher.

"We are told that they used this road," answered the middle-aged man. "In fact, a book in the library shows a map indicating a hotel in this area where the coaches stopped overnight. They didn't travel at night in those days unless it was necessary."

"Look what I found," called one of the boys racing back to the road from a nearby field. "It's an arrowhead."

Upon reaching the road, he was immediately surrounded by several of the children.

"It *is* an arrowhead, Mr. Bently," said another boy holding it up for his teacher to see. "Let's look for arrowheads. There should be more of them here. If Jimmy found one, I can find one too."

Tom Bently took the piece of flint in his hand. "That sure is an arrowhead, kids. This area was known to have a large settlement of Indians at one time."

Nearly everyone in the Sunday School class began searching for arrowheads, heading in various directions.

"Listen, gang," called Tom, "don't wander out of sight. Stay where I can see you. Be careful and watch out for snakes."

Tom had no sooner spoken the warning when one of

the girls screamed. She grabbed her leg as she continued to cry out.

"Snake! It bit me. Mr. Bently, help!"

Tom ran to the little girl who was sitting on the ground holding her left leg. Lifting her hands, he saw the fang marks just below her knee.

Tom acted quickly. He fastened a hastily-made tourniquet around her leg above the knee. He took his snake-bite kit from his pocket and quickly made a deep incision over each fang mark. The top of the rubber kit case served as a suction cup. The little girl was too scared to notice the pain from the cuts made in her leg.

"Just relax, Judy," said Tom kindly. "Its fang marks are close together. I think it's a small snake."

Just then, one of the boys lifted a flat rock to find the snake. "There it is, Mr. Bently. It's a green snake."

The Sunday School teacher, who walked often in the woods and had studied about the animals and reptiles, glanced at the small snake.

"Is that the snake you saw, Judy?" he asked, pointing to the reptile which was lying perfectly still.

"That's the snake, Mr. Bently. I was kneeling down right there when it bit me."

Tom smiled. "That snake is not poisonous, honey. You probably kneeled on it and scared it."

The teacher then surprised the children by reaching down and picking up the green snake. "Now don't you children do this. You have to know how to hold them and, too, you may pick up one that is poisonous." He then placed the snake back on the ground and saw it disappear under a rock.

"I'm sorry, Judy, that I had to hurt you. You see, that is what I would have had to do to save your life had the snake been poisonous."

He picked Judy up in his arms. "Let's go, kids. I want Dr. Jones to look at Judy's leg. He's going to have to bandage up the cuts that I made."

The children, including Judy, laughed at their Sunday School teacher's remarks. All were happy, knowing their friend was going to be all right.

Judy's mother came out the front door as Tom's car turned into the driveway. He had called her from the doctor's office, assuring her that everything was all right with her daughter.

The teacher carried Judy into the house and placed her on the living room sofa. He visited a few minutes and then excused himself to drop off the other children at their homes.

"I like Mr. Bently, Mommy," reported Judy, watching his car back out of the driveway. "He was worried about me until he saw the snake."

"Thank the Lord it was not poisonous," spoke Judy's mother more to herself than to Judy.

"Oh, Mommy!" cried Judy, "I'm so scared. I could have died today. I could be dead right now!"

"Well, you aren't, honey," spoke her mother, putting her arms around the little girl. "Don't even think of what could have happened. You are well and safe."

"But, Mommy," sobbed Judy, "I have to think of it. I'm not a Christian like you and Daddy. I told Mr. Bently that I was a Christian, but I'm not one."

Her little body shook from her crying. "Please pray with me, Mommy. Please help me. I want Jesus to live in my heart."

The mother and daughter bowed their heads as Judy asked God to forgive her sins and save her. When she finished praying, she smiled through the tears and put both arms around her mother.

"I'm glad that snake bit me today, Mommy," continued Judy. "It made me stop pretending to be a Christian. I'm a real Christian now."

She hugged her mother as she spoke, "When Mr. Bently comes to see me tonight, I have a surprise for him—a real big surprise."

That evening, Tom stopped off to see Judy. She was sitting in a big easy chair when he walked in.

"Hello, Mr. Bently," she greeted him with a big smile.

"Hi, Judy. How are you feeling?" asked the teacher.

"I feel fine," she answered. "I'm glad that snake wasn't poisonous. I might not be here tonight."

"Oh, I think you would still be here," replied Tom. "I put the tourniquet on right away and made those incisions. Of course, you wouldn't be this well, but I think you would still be here."

"Now," continued Tom, "let's take a look at what I brought for you."

He reached into his pocket and brought out a small bag which he handed to Judy. She took it and thanked him. Slowly she opened it.

"Arrowheads!" she called out. "Look Mommy and Daddy! I have my own arrowheads."

She reached into the bag and pulled out a handful of plastic bags, each holding one arrowhead.

"There are five of them. Oh, thank you, Mr. Bently. They're beautiful."

Tom then told them how he had started a collection when he was Judy's age. "I must have nearly six hundred of them."

There was a moment of silence and then Judy spoke. "Mr. Bently, I have a surprise for you. Something wonderful happened after you left this afternoon."

"What is the surprise, Judy?" asked the kind teacher, smiling.

"Mommy and I were talking about what happened to me," spoke the happy little girl. "I told Mommy that maybe if it was a poisonous snake, I might not be here with her anymore. I told her I wasn't sure of being with Jesus either."

The Sunday School teacher listened without saying a word.

"I asked Mommy to pray with me. I asked Jesus to come into my heart, Mr. Bently," said Judy in her soft voice.

Tom reached out and put his arm around the girl. "I'm so happy, Judy. Thank you for that nice surprise. Isn't it wonderful how the Lord takes some of the most unpleasant experiences and turns them into blessings?"

Judy's conversion and the arrowheads became the main topics of conversation for the next thirty minutes.

That night Tom prayed beside his bed, "Thank You,

Father, for Your watchcare over the children today. Thank You that the snake was not poisonous and that Judy's life was spared to become Your child."

THE REASON WHY

IT IS GOOD FOR ME THAT I HAVE BEEN AFFLICTED; THAT I MIGHT KNOW THY STATUTES (Ps. 119:71).

The sound of crashing underbrush startled Rama, one of seven children, whose parents farmed a small piece of land to supplement their income. The garden was nearly a mile from their home and bordered a dense jungle which was home for wild animals and snakes. Rama never knew what might come out of that jungle.

The young Indian looked up to see a ferocious Bengal tiger standing about twenty feet away. The huge cat fixed its eyes on Rama, who tried to scare it off with his three-foot garden hoe. The tiger took several quick steps forward and then leaped on the frightened Indian, sending him to the ground. Sharp fangs pierced Rama's shoulder. The pain seemed unbearable. Then Rama lost consciousness.

"Rama!" came a voice off in the distance. "Rama, can you hear me?"

The son of the Indian farmer tried to focus his eyes on the blurred figure standing by him. A bright light shone in his face. Partly conscious, he felt as though he had fallen into a deep well and was slowly floating toward the top.

"Rama, do you hear me? Can you see my hand?" came the voice again. In desperation, Rama tried to focus his eyes. Whoever was talking to him was dressed in green.

"I . . . I . . . can . . . see . . . you," whispered Rama. "I . . . see you."

In a few minutes the blurred face became clear, and Rama realized that he was in a hospital. A doctor and three nurses stood beside him.

"What happened?" he asked as his mind and vision cleared. "How did I get here? Who are you?"

"I am Dr. Reid, Rama," answered the man standing over him. "You were attacked by a tiger and were carried here to the mission hospital by your father. He found you in the garden."

"What did the tiger do to me?" Rama asked.

The missionary doctor smiled, then told his concerned patient, "It bit you on your right shoulder. You also have some claw marks on your arms, chest and legs. You don't have any broken bones, but we will have to keep you here for a few days."

Rama closed his eyes as he spoke. "I'm glad to be alive," he whispered. "I could have been killed."

"Our God spared your life," added Dr. Reid.

Two nurses wheeled their newest patient to the recovery room. "The doctor will be in to see you later," one of them told Rama. "If you need us, just push that button there on your bed."

In about an hour, Dr. Reid went to the recovery room to check on his patient. Rama greeted him as he entered.

"Hello, Doctor. I'm glad to have you stop by. I have something to ask you."

"You're looking better already, Rama," the physician commented. "What is it that you want to ask me?"

The teenage Indian's face reflected the seriousness of the question. "What did you mean when you said your God spared my life? Your God doesn't even know me."

"Oh yes, He does, Rama," responded Dr. Reid quickly. "He knows all about you. He loves you, too, and did something for you so you can live forever with Him."

Rama was surprised to hear such words from his new friend. "You mean your God loves me and can make me live forever?"

The Christian doctor then told the young man how God the Father sent His Son to this world to die for the sins of the human race. He explained how anyone anywhere can call upon Christ to save him. When he finished, Rama reached out with his bandaged arm to the missionary.

"Dr. Reid, now I know why that tiger attacked me. That wasn't any mistake. I would not have been able to hear these good words about your God and His Son, Jesus."

Dr. Reid took Rama's hand as the Indian continued, "Will you help me to know your God, Doctor, like you do?"

Within seconds the patient and physician bowed their heads as Rama received Christ as his Savior. After both had prayed, Dr. Reid opened the Bible which he had taken from his carrying case.

"I want to read you something from God's Book, Rama."

He then read from Psalm 119:71, "It is good for me that I have been afflicted; that I might know thy statutes."

"That's me, Doctor," said Rama, smiling. "That's me in that Book. Our God knew all about me even before I knew Him."

Rama could hardly wait until his family would be allowed to see him. He had some good news to tell them about God the Father and His Son, Jesus. And, too, he just had to tell them about God's Book and how it gave the reason why he had been attacked by the tiger and brought to the hospital where he came to know the true God.